Between Reality and Unreality

I0562118

Iris Carden

Between Reality and Unreality

Published by Iris Carden
   Ipswich, Qld, Australia
   iriscardenauthor.blog

ISBN: 978-0-6459679-8-2

A catalogue record for this work is available from the National Library of Australia.

Cover Art: The Border by Iris Carden

This is the first book in the Witch and Wisp series

Contents:

Lost and Found

People might have called Orsinius Wishlet a kleptomaniac, if they had known about him. But nobody did so nobody could call him anything. Orsinius was a wisp, living on the cusp of Reality and Unreality, not entirely here, but not completely not there.

People might have called Orsinius Wishlet a hoarder, had they seen his burrow. But as humans cannot see the fine barrier between what is and what isn't, or whatever is or is not inside that barrier, nobody called him anything at all.

Today Orsinius had a new treasure.

As Maryanne Heggarty frantically searched under a chest of drawers for one diamond earring which she had dropped while removing it from her ear, Orsinius was carrying that sparkly object past his front door.

Near the front door was a pile of papers: hundreds of newspaper clippings people had cut to remember precious events, but then misplaced; thousands of shopping lists and telephone messages; a great idea for a novel that would never be written; the cheque that Angela Fromington insisted she had put in the mail, but the collections company claimed not to have received; and little Kerry Softmore's Christmas card to her beloved grandmother.

While Maryanne Heggarty got a torch in hopes the light would be reflected in the facets of her missing diamond, Orsinius passed his biro store. There were biros of every colour, and every value. There were cheap Bics that had been left beside the phone for messages, institutional looking pens that still had chains attached to them which were meant to stop them going missing from bank or post office benches. There were more upmarket pens that had rolled off desks, disappeared in the bottom of handbags, or from desk drawers. There was even an engraved gold pen, given as a gift to the politician in appreciation of his kindness to a particular business organisation.

While Maryanne tried to explain to her husband how one of the pair of earrings he'd given for her for their anniversary had simply vanished into thin air, Orsinius climbed over the jumble that formed his bed. Mostly this pile was odd socks, lost from washing machines, from under beds or from kids sports bags. There were also a number of teddy bears and other soft toys, and Orsinius flinched has he stepped on the knitting needle still in the half-made jumper Gertrude Durnsteff had just put down for a moment while she checked the mail.

As the Heggartys searched their bedroom, both exclaiming it could not have gone far, Orsinius moved aside his card collection. There were bank debit cards and credit cards, access cards for secure doors, endless shop loyalty cards, the business card of the plumber who'd actually turned up on time and done the job well for the quoted price, all sorts of bits of plastic and cardboard that humans had carried in handbags or wallets or left stuck on the fridge.

As the Heggartys' frustration led to an argument, Orsinius finally reached the deepest, most special section of his burrow. This was where his greatest, shiniest, treasures lay. Very gently, he lay the diamond alongside a various items of highly polished silverware, a tiara from a European royal house, an historic necklace from a museum display, a Faberge egg and ruby the size of a golf ball.

As Martin Heggarty slammed the door and left his wife in tears, Orsinius sat transfixed, looking at the shining and glittering things in the deepest part of his burrow, on the boarder between Reality and Unreality.

A Wish Come True

Ariana looked around her. She was tired, but everything was perfect.

Even her parents, who hardly had a civil word for each other normally, were happily dancing together.

She looked down at her shiny new wedding ring. At last she and Jack had done it. They were married, and were planning to live happily ever after. She couldn't see where Jack was just at that moment but he was surely circulating among the guests, being congratulated.

On the table beside her was the wishing well. Martha, her sister, her bridesmaid, had made it for her. Instead of gifts, guests put money into the wishing well, to start their bank account for saving their house deposit. The little "well" was beautiful, carefully constructed from brightly-painted balsa wood, with ribbons and bows and flowers over it, in a manner only someone as artistic as Martha could have made look so elegant and beautiful. On the side was written, "To Ariana and Jack. May all your wishes come true."

Ariana gently touched a satin bow as she admired her sister's artwork. She looked at the dance floor, and realised that all of the people she loved most in the world were together tonight and having a wonderful time. "I wish this moment could last for ever," she murmured.

Suddenly, everything stopped. Dancers stopped mid-step. Everything around her was frozen - a strange tableau of a wedding celebration.

Ariana walked over to her parents. They were totally still, like something from a waxworks museum.

Her Uncle Fred was suspended mid-air, caught in the midst of falling from his chair after drinking more champagne than he really could handle. (Knowing Uncle Fred, he probably started celebrating long before the actual wedding ceremony.)

A bartender was pouring a beer - the liquid frozen mid pour.

Ariana wasn't the only one moving. A small, bald, man with a grey beard was putting items of cutlery into a basket. She didn't know him and was sure he wasn't on the guest list.

"Who are you?" She asked.

"You can see me? But you're a human. Humans cannot see me."

"I can see you. Who are you? If you're not human what are you?"

"I am Orsinius Wishlet. I am a wisp."

"And why can't humans usually see you?"

"I do not exist. Well, I do, but I do not. You understand?"

"Not at all. Why is no-one else moving?"

"They are. But this is the Interim."

"The what?"

"The Interim. Between the tick and the tock. Between moment and moment. We are outside of time."

"Outside of ... How did this happen?"

"Well, I use the Interim to build my collection, and avoid humans. I do not know why you are in it." He took an icing flower from the wedding cake and added it to his basket.

"I just touched the wishing well here, and I wished the moment would last for ever."

Orsinius climbed on the table beside the wishing well. On his hands and knees he carefully took a $50 note from the wishing well, avoiding touching the well itself, and then sniffed the well. "Smells like magic." He said, "Strong magic. I advise not touching it."

"But I already did touch it. And that money you just took was part of my wedding present!"

"Oh yes. I have many of these in my collection. Thank you. I have enough now. I will return to my burrow."

"Your burrow? Where is that?"

"On the border."

"Border?"

"The border between Reality and Unreality."

"The border between Reality and Unreality? That's a thing?"

"It is and it is not. Reality is a thing, but Unreality is not."

"Of course. Do you know how I get out if this Interim thingy?"

"I do not know. I know how I get in and out of it, but I do not know how a human would. I have to go. Humans are frightening and talking to you is making me feel anxious." With that he simply disappeared.

"I'm in the Interim between the tick and the tock, I've been talking to a creature that lives on the border between Reality and Unreality. I'm clearly either dreaming or going insane." Ariana said to herself, and took a deep breath.

She couldn't see Jack in the reception hall, and went looking for him. Just outside, she found him. Frozen mid-kiss with Martha. It wasn't a congratulatory peck on the cheek between a new brother-in-law and sister-in-law. It was a full-fledged lover's kiss.

This was horrifying, even more so than being outside of time, while all of the people she cared about were frozen.

Back in the reception hall, she tried touching people, shaking their shoulders, pinching them, trying to get someone to move, to notice her. Nobody moved or responded in any way.

Touching the wishing well again she said, "I wish I'd never made that wish." Nothing happened.

She was stuck. Surrounded by all the people she loved and cared about, she was totally alone.

Sweet Sixteen

The cupcakes had cooled, so I cut the tops off, and halved them. I filled the cakes with jam and whipped cream, then put the halves of the tops back as wings, and dusted them all with icing sugar.

Andy wanted butterfly cakes for her 16th birthday. I wanted her to have exactly what she wanted. Her life was about to change in so many dramatic ways, and I wanted to help her hold on to the innocence just a little longer.

I reached for the birthday candles, but they weren't there. I had a wisp problem, obviously. I reached into the Interim, that space between moments, and pulled the small miscreant out by his overlarge ear.

"Orsinius Wishlet," I said. "Of course it had to be you. This is not a good day to annoy me."

"Oh sorry, Your Ladyship," he said with a bow, as nervous sweat beaded his over-large bald head. "If you could tell me when a good day would be, I could come back then."

"Do you know what today is?" I asked.

"Friday?" he said hopefully.

"Actually, it's Saturday, and it's also my daughter's sixteenth birthday."

"Congratulations, Your Ladyship," he said, followed by, "Oh."

"Oh indeed. This is the last birthday before her powers start to come in and her wings start to grow. This is the birthday when I have to tell her who and what we are and what we do. So don't mess with me today. And give me those candles."

He handed over the candles. "I'm sorry, Your Ladyship, I could not help myself. You know I just see things and want them for my collection. Those are especially nice birthday candles, too."

"They are especially nice candles for my daughter, not for you. What are you doing in my house anyway?"

"Sadly, Your Ladyship," here, he bowed again, "I am here to report a malicious misuse of magic."

I put candles in individual butterfly cakes, "So you want to report your cousin Augustus for using the Interim to steal from humans?"

"No! I would never report Augustus!"

"I don't see why not," I said as I arranged the cakes on a stand. "He reports you twice a week. You're both lucky I can't be bothered hunting down wisps."

"I appreciate your graciousness in that matter, Your Ladyship, but I am here to report a much, much more serious matter."

I turned from the cakes to look at him. What kind of trouble could the miniature kleptomaniac have got himself into? "OK," I said, "so report this misuse of magic."

"There is a human trapped in the Interim!" he almost squealed it.

"There's what? How did a human get in the Interim?"

"Magic," he said. "Strong magic. I smelled it. It was a wishing spell."

"A wishing spell? Who would be dumb enough to play with those?"

There hadn't been a case of a wishing spell cast since my great-grandmother's time. They were so dangerous no magical creature would dare use one. Of course, a human could have come across an old grimoire and fancied themself a witch. Humans did the stupidest things when they encountered magic.

"It was a wishing spell in a wishing well," Orsinius explained.

"Gotta love the classics. Right, show me where to find this trapped human and the wishing well with the spell. I'll deal with those first."

I put the cakes in the fridge, then opened the secret cupboard, taking out my scimitar and dagger. I said, "And then I'll deal with whoever cast that spell."

After today, I would have to begin taking Andromeda on cases like this. Just one more day of butterfly cakes and innocence.

The humans have it wrong. Justice doesn't have a blindfold and carry scales. Lady Justice has a five metre wingspan and carries a razor-sharp ancestral sword.

A Sanctioned Theft

Orsinius Wishlet slept badly. His bed, made of socks and other lost soft fabrics, contained a piece of half-finished knitting complete with knitting needle. This night, no matter how often he changed position, he found the needle was sticking him.

When he finally did fall asleep, he was exhausted and his mind gave him fearful and terrible dreams. He dreamt of a terrible curved sword removing the head of a criminal. Then he dreamed of the sword coming for his head.

Orsinius woke to bright sunlight, in a strange place. He was in the middle of a large circle of giant stones. Some of the stones were stacked on others. He wasn't alone. There was a tall old man beside him. The man had long white hair and a white beard, both hanging below his waist. Orsinius could smell magic, stronger magic than he had ever smelled.

"Good morning Mr Wishlet," the old man said. "I presume you know who I am?"

Orsinius thought. His tired brain struggled a moment and then produced the name. He said, "You are the great Merlin, Sir."

"Correct, Mr Wishlet. I have brought you here because I have a quest for you."

"For me? Oh no, Sir, you must be mistaken. I am not an adventurer who goes on quests. I am just a wisp, and I must confess, until today I have been a thief."

The old wizard smiled. "Ah, but a thief is exactly who I need for this quest. I need a very special item stolen."

Orsinius shook his head, then grasped it in both his hands. For the first time he realised how attached he was to his head, and how much he wanted it to stay on his neck. "Sorry Sir," he said, trembling. "I am a reformed thief today. Lady Justice has told me she is getting tired of wisps stealing. I will resist the urge to take things I want now."

"This is a sanctioned theft, Mr Wishlet." Merlin said, "Lady Justice herself recommended you for it. She told me of your courage and audacity to steal from her house right in front of her. That's the kind of courage and skill I need at this moment."

"Lady Justice recommended me?" Orsinius thought of her razor sharp curved sword. "I will do whatever her Ladyship chooses, then and what you choose, of course, too Sir."

"Excellent." Merlin said. "Not far from here is an archaeological dig. That's when humans dig up old things, to try to understand their ancestors. I can't see the value of that myself. I lived with their ancestors and didn't understand them most of the time. Among the things the archaeologists have found is a magical artefact. It's far too powerful and dangerous to be in human hands. I know, because I once made the mistake of putting it in human hands. That human, admittedly, was exceptional."

"You want me to steal this object, and bring it to you?" Orsinius asked.

"No. I want you to steal the object and take it somewhere the humans can't possibly get it. Lady Justice tells me you make your burrow on the border between Reality and Unreality."

"Yes, I do."

"Good. That's an excellent place to store it. No human will ever find it there."

"You want me to keep a dangerous magical object in my home?"

"It will not harm you if you don't misuse it. If you just store it with your valuables, it will be safe. If your try to use it for evil or selfish purposes, it will destroy you."

Orsinius shook his head. He could see this going horribly wrong. "I do not know. It sounds like a grave responsibility. I am just a wisp. I cannot be guardian to such a dangerous magical object."

"You can and you must," Merlin said. "I have seen your future, Mr Wishlet, and you will indeed be guardian of Excalibur. Tomorrow you will discover you are much more than you believe you are today."

"Tomorrow? What is happening tomorrow?"

"I mean 'tomorrow' figuratively, to indicate the future, not specifically the day after today. Although the day after today will also bring you surprises. Now, I am going to the archaeological dig. I am going to talk to the people working there. I will point to the object I want stolen. You will use the Interim to take it."

Orsinius was very familiar with the Interim, that time between moments. It was the tool he'd used to steal most of the objects in his collection, without humans being aware of his presence.

He dutifully followed Merlin to the dig site, and hid to watch as one of the workers greeted the wizard.

"Dr Merle, great to see you again! I'm sure you want to see our great discovery," the man said.

"Yes, Dr Algester, from your description on the phone, I'm sure it's quite something. I really didn't want to wait for it to arrive at the museum."

"It's in our site office now. Right this way."

Orsinius slipped from behind a rock, to behind a tree, following as the human and wizard entered a caravan. He waited a few moments and then entered the Interim, before following. Inside, frozen in time, the human and wizard were standing looking at a jewelled cup. Merlin, with hands behind his back, was pointing to an object on the table behind them.

16

That object was a sword. Unlike the scimitar he had seen Lady Justice wield the day before, this was a straight sword, and looked very plain. There were no jewels in the hilt, just some odd symbols engraved on the blade. He could, however, smell the magic radiating from it. It was almost as strong as the magic scent coming from Merlin himself. Orsinius now remembered where he had heard the word "Excalibur" before.

He had never been nervous about a theft before, but he was anxious as he picked up the mysterious sword. As soon as it was in his hand, he darted back to his burrow, back to the very deepest part, where he stored rare jewels. He very carefully placed the sword amongst his most precious treasures.

Now what? Should he polish it as he did with his other treasures? Would that be the correct way to show respect to such a powerful object. He decided that he should explain himself, in case the sword would misunderstand his intent.

"Great Excalibur," he said, "I know you have been lost in the earth a very long time. With your permission, I will clean and polish you and try to bring you back to your former glory. If this is the wrong thing to do I apologise. I only wish to show the greatest respect."

He found a soft cloth from his bed, brought it to his treasure-space and carefully polished the sword. As the sword began to gleam, it also seemed to grow warm in his hands. Warm and comfortable, as if it was content to be with him.

An Unexpected Visitor

Orsinius Wishlet had had a very long and tiring day. He had recently given up being a thief, but, having no other skills or experience, was finding it difficult to find food.

Today, he had found several mushrooms, of dubious edibility, some berries and a half eaten hamburger he'd found in a bin. It was only late this day that he'd decided that taking things from bins was technically not stealing, because it was things humans had already thrown away. He was quite sure Lady Justice would not execute him for taking food from bins. Having come to this conclusion, he had high hopes that he would eat quite well the next day.

As he carried his groceries into his burrow, he immediately noticed some things had been disturbed. His pile of papers had been disturbed, papers in all the wrong places, newspaper clippings, lost cheques, birthday cards, shopping lists, all of which had been placed according to his own organisational system were now out of place.

Who had been in his burrow? What else had they disturbed? What might they have taken?

Orsinius, very worried and quite frightened, went further in. His biro store was not the nice neat mountain of missing pens that he had left, but a chaotic mass of pens spread far and wide.

He wondered for a moment if whoever had done this was still in his home. Should he run and get Lady Justice to protect him. It was her job to protect innocent people from criminals, and he was no longer a criminal. Then he remembered the task Lady Justice and the Great Wizard Merlin had entrusted to him. He could not go and seek help, because if the item he was meant to be guarding had gone, then he would be in trouble.

He gulped hard at the thought of both of those powerful beings being angry with him. Then he courageously, fearfully, walked deeper into his burrow. His bed, made of odd socks, lost knitting and other soft textiles was in utter disarray.

He went further in, to the very deepest part of his burrow, the place where he kept all his most precious and shiny objects, the place where he kept that object.

There he found his cousin Augustus.

Augustus was rummaging through his most precious things!

"What are you doing?" Orsinius asked, quite shocked. His cousin was a thief, but would never steal from him, or would he?

"I know it is here somewhere. I want it." Augustus said in a demanding tone.

"You want what?" Orsinius asked, confused.

"Everyone knows the Great Wizard Merlin gave a a precious thing to you. I want that thing."

"Do you even know what that thing is?" Orsinius wondered why Augustus would want such a terrible responsibility.

"I do not care what it is!" Augustus said. "When I heard that you had been given something so special and I had not, my heart made thumping noises, my brain yelled at me, 'Orsinius is just a thief. Orsinius is no more worthy than me!' And I knew a mistake had been made and I was meant to have the thing."

"But you are also just a thief, and I am no longer one," Orsinius said, quite reasonably.

Augustus picked up Orsinius' prized Faberge egg. "This looks valuable. Is this the thing?"

Orsinius considered lying and saying it was, then thought that reformed thieves probably should not lie, "I cannot say,." he said.

Augustus picked up a golf-ball sized ruby. Orsinius' heart almost broke to think his cousin might take that from him.

Then August sniffed. He sniffed again. With a terrible sinking feeling, Orsinius realised his cousin had smelled the magic.

Throwing the ruby aside, August picked up an old sword from the back of the pile.

"This is it. This old sword that stinks of magic. This is what Merlin gave you. This is mine now. I will take it and keep it where you can't find it."

"No," said Orsinius, "you must not do that. The Great Merlin said it must be respected and if you do evil with it, like stealing it, bad things will happen."

"Who are you to tell me what I can and cannot do?" Augustus demanded.

"I am your cousin." Orsinius answered, "I am a wisp. I am a former thief." He sounded a little bolder as he said, "I am chosen by Lady Justice and the Great Wizard Merlin." He pulled himself up to his full 135 centimetre height and stuck out his chest, held out his hand and said, "I am Orsinius Wishlet, Guardian of Excalibur!"

The sward twisted in Augustus' hand, pulled away, and flew into Orsinius' outstretched hand.

"Augustus," he said. "You have reported me to Lady Justice many times, but until now I have not reported you. If you do not leave my burrow immediately or if you ever come back, I will report you for the attempted theft of Excalibur. You know you will not survive her revenge. Go. Do not come back."

Augustus looked at his cousin, who suddenly seemed so strong and so authoritative, and he turned to run out of the burrow, stumbling on the way.

Orsinius carefully polished the sword and put it back in its place. He remembered Merlin telling him, "Who you are today is not who you will be tomorrow." He began to wonder who he was going to become.

Finding a Friend

Orsinius Wishlet was walking down a busy city street, when he heard a voice call out, "Orsinius? Is that you? Orsinius Wishlet?"

He turned to see a human woman running toward him. Other humans had stopped to see what the yelling was about. Humans could see him? All humans could see him? So much had changed recently, that he couldn't find the energy to be surprised.

"Do you remember me?" The woman asked as she approached, "Ariana Sutton, well, I was Jones for about five minutes, but I've gone back to my own name." She leaned in and whispered, "The woman who as stuck in the Interim."

Orsinius now remembered her. It had not really been that long ago, but so much had happened since then. He had found her trapped in the Interim, the time between the tick and the tock, between moments, unable to get out.

"I didn't get the chance to thank you," she said. "If you hadn't brought the scary lady with the wings to save me, I guess I would still be there."

Orsinius thought she would be dead by now, given that she had been stuck in a frozen moment of time.

"Can I buy you a coffee?" She asked

All Orsinius knew of coffee was that it was a mildly magical liquid that seemed to make humans happy. He had never drunk it before, but was willing to try. So he agreed.

The woman led him to a coffee shop, and since he didn't know anything about coffee she bought for both of them.

Orsinius tried very hard to think of an appropriate thing to say to this human who was really the only human he'd ever actually spoken to. "I am sorry about your sister," he said.

"So am I," she said. "But I guess she'd broken some kind of magical law. Even though I didn't know magic had laws, and she probably didn't either, she definitely knew what she was doing was wrong. It was a shock to see…" Ariana shuddered.

"Yes, it was," Orsinius agreed, remembering that terrible sword.

"I do miss her, you know, even though she had an affair with my husband, well he's not my husband now, and tried to lock me away in time for ever. Even so, she was still my sister."

Orsinius nodded. He understood. He missed his cousin Augustus, even though he'd had to threaten Augustus with that very same fate Ariana's sister had suffered.

"I'm still so incredibly grateful to you," Ariana continued. "If there's every anything I can do for you. I know I'm only human, and you're this amazing magical creature, but if there is anything I can do, please just ask."

Orsinius had a thought. There was something he could ask. He said, "When we met, I was a thief. I was there to steal things when I met you. Since then I have stopped being a thief." He thought of that flashing sword again. He went on. "But I do not know how to not be a thief. I have found some food in rubbish bins, but I am very hungry. Can you tell me how humans get food?"

When their coffees arrived, Ariana ordered a meal for herself, and invited Orsinius to choose what he wanted. "I'm buying," she said.

Once the waitress was out of earshot, Ariana said, "Well, first you need a job."

"A job?" Orsinius was sure he didn't have one of those in his collection.

"A job is when you do something someone else wants done, and they give you money for it."

23

"I know what money is." Orsinius said, "I have some in my collection. Some of it is very pretty."

"Well, you use the money to go to a shop and buy food."

"A job will give me money and money will give me food," Orsinius summarised. "How do I find this job?"

"I can help you there," Ariana said. "I'm a hairdresser. I can give you a job sweeping up hair and making coffee for my customers."

"I do not know how to do those things," Orsinius admitted, sadly. "I really don't know how to do anything except steal things."

"It's OK. I'll teach you. And I'll teach you how to do your shopping and buy your food and everything else you need."

The waitress brought their meals.

While they ate, Ariana asked, "Orsinius, back in the Interim, you said something about being not quite real, or not really existing or something similar, and being surprised I could see you. But now, everyone seems to be able to see you. The waitress just put your plate in front of you without seeming to think anything was odd. Do you think, maybe, you've become or are becoming more real?"

Orsinius thought. "Many strange things have been happening to me recently," he said. "I stopped being a thief. Someone very important asked me to do an important thing. I even stood up to my cousin Augustus. These are things I never would have imagined would happen. So perhaps another strange thing is happening as well. Perhaps I am becoming real."

"That's exciting," Ariana said, "and being real will definitely help you with the whole working and buying your own food and things. I'm sure everything is going to work out for you Orsinius, and I will help you with anything I can. I owe you everything."

A strange thought began to form in Orsinius' mind. "Ariana, are we friends?" He asked.

"Orsinius," she answered, "you're the best friend I've ever had."

Orsinius sighed. He had a job. He was going to buy food for himself and not steal it. He had a friend, when he'd never had a friend before. The friend was human, but he was sure she still counted. And he was becoming real.

The Old Cup

Orsinius Wishlet was sweeping the hairdressing salon floor, when he heard the ding of the bell that said the door had been opened.

Without looking up from his task he said, "Ariana is finished for the day, but I can make you an appointment for tomorrow if you like."

"I don't need an appointment," a frighteningly familiar voice answered.

Looking up, he saw someone he really did not want to see.

Lady Justice looked down at him.

"Your Ladyship," he stammered as he bowed, his bald head gleaming with anxious sweat, and his grey beard brushing the floor.

While he was looking at the floor, the bell dinged again, and the strong smell of magic told him before he looked up that his next visitor was Merlin.

Orsinius stood up straight again, just as his employer walked out of the back room saying, "Everything's in the steriliser, and the coffee maker's cleaned up, so when you're done sweeping we can call it a day."

She stopped short, and gulped as she looked at the visitors. Lady Justice she had encountered before, but then the tall imposing woman had large wings and was carrying a sword.

"I had heard about this, but I really didn't believe it," Lady Justice said. "Orsinius Wishlet doing a normal human job. So you really did give up your life of crime?"

Orsinius bowed again. "Yes, My Lady," he said. "You said you were growing tired of wisps committing thefts, so I gave up being a thief. But I did not know how to live without stealing, so my friend Ariana gave me this job and taught me how to use money to buy food."

Lady Justice looked at the human woman. "You've done this wisp a great service," she said.

Ariana found her voice, "Orsinius did me a great service by saving my life, or at least by getting you to come and save my life. And I don't think it was very fair to expect him to give up stealing when he didn't know how to get a job or even how to shop for food or anything."

Suddenly, Ariana remembered the razor-sharp scimitar this woman had used to exact justice against her sister, and decided it was better to stop talking.

Lady Justice laughed. "You're absolutely right," she said. "I should not have expected so much of Orsinius without giving him some instruction or help in how to live a crime-free life. In my defence, however, I didn't actually expect any such thing. I believed he would just go on as normal. I've given his cousin numerous such warnings without any effect."

"Well," said Ariana quietly, "Orsinius is just a good person, is all. I can't say anything about his cousin. I don't know him." Ariana tried to stop her eyes from staring at Lady Justice's shoulders, but was unable to do so.

"It's a glamour," Lady Justice told her. "A spell. I use it to prevent people seeing my wings most of the time. Wings attract too much of the wrong type of attention.

The tall, white-haired man who had been standing behind Lady Justice stepped forward and offered his hand for her to shake, "Hello Miss Sutton. I'm Merlin, and I would like to thank you for your assistance to Mr Wishlet. Discovering the magical world can be quite intimidating to humans, and it was brave of you to offer to help."

"Merlin... as in..."

Merlin nodded.

Ariana found herself unable to think or speak for a moment or two. She was holding the proffered hand, forgetting to let go.

Merlin, ignoring that a dumbstruck human was standing like a statue holding his hand, turned his attention to Orsinius. "Mr Wishlet, I have heard about the recent incident with your cousin. I know that Excalibur itself has affirmed its allegiance to you. You are exactly who I believed you to be. And because of that, I have another, equally important task for you."

"Excalibur?" Ariana said faintly, as she finally managed to let go of the wizard's hand.

From a fold of his robes, Merlin extracted a very old, very dusty, wooden cup.

"This doesn't look like much," Merlin said, "but it is vitally important that it doesn't fall into the wrong hands. I believe the chosen guardian of Excalibur is the best person to be responsible for it."

Orsinius accepted the cup, cautiously. It smelled strongly of something like magic, but not the same as any magic he had smelled before.

"We thank you for your great service," Merlin said, and then turned to leave.

"Wait!" Orsinius said. "I have to ask you something. You once said who I was was not who I would be. And now humans can see me. Am I becoming something else?"

The wizard turned back to face him, "Mr Wishlet, humans could always see you. You were just very good at hiding from them, especially with the extensive use you made of the Interim. As for who you are becoming, that is about your character, your destiny, not your species. And you are well on the way to becoming who you will be. Your destiny is far more important than that of any wisp before you, or likely after you."

Merlin turned again and opened the door, then instead of walking through it, simply vanished, leaving the door to swing closed again and the bell to ding. His voice, seemingly left behind, said, "I do like your doorbell, Miss Sutton."

Lady Justice said, "Actually, I do need an appointment to have my hair done, and one for my daughter as well, but I think this has all been a bit overwhelming for both of you, so I'll phone about it tomorrow."

She left, using the door in the normal manner.

Orsinius and Ariana both stood looking at the cup.

Things started to click together in Ariana's mind.

"Merlin.. Excalibur... You know what this cup is, don't you Orsinius?

Orsinius' mind hadn't quite worked through the links yet. He shook his overlarge head.

"It's a wooden cup, like a carpenter might have. Merlin had it. Merlin was part of King Arthur's court. You have Excalibur, King Arthur's sword. You know what all of King Arthur's court was always looking for? A cup! A cup that had been owned by a carpenter. Orsinius, you're holding the Holy Grail."

Orsinius almost dropped the cup.

"What am I supposed to do with this?" he said quietly.

"What did you do with Excalibur?"

"I hid it in my burrow, with my most precious things."

"I guess you put the Grail there too."

"Then what?"

"Then we go to the library and learn everything we can about these things Merlin has you looking after."

Orsinius nodded. His previous experience with libraries had only been to steal books, and he had no idea how to actually find information from one, but he realised Ariana would know how.

The Rip

Orsinius Wishlet was sitting in the break room at his work. He had recently learned how to make coffee, a soup of mildly magical beans. He'd made one each for himself and his friend and boss Ariana.

He took a mouthful of the coffee. Its magic was very mild, but it was enough that it made humans happy, and he had developed a taste for it. Harmless magic was a rare experience for him.

"It's been a really long day," Ariana sighed. "Since all the magical beings started coming here, we've been flat out. I might have to hire another hairdresser. But how would we explain our customers to them?"

Orsinius shrugged his shoulders, as he had seen humans do when they didn't have an answer to a question. Ariana had only discovered the magical world when she'd been trapped in a cruel magical spell. She'd met Orsinius when he'd found her and arranged her rescue.

"Oh, I know you have a much bigger problem than being overworked," Ariana continued. "Do you have any idea what you're meant to do with the... things?"

He shook his head. Merlin had entrusted him with both Excalibur, and with an old cup that both he and Ariana suspected of being the Holy Grail. It was a big responsibility for a wisp, and a former thief. He had no idea what he was meant to do with them. They were safely stored in his burrow, on the border between Reality and Unreality.

Ariana was about to speak again, when there was a sudden, very loud sound, like fabric ripping, but as loud as a jet engine.

They both left their coffees and went outside. On the street in front of the hairdressing salon, they found chaos. Some people were running, some were standing and staring. A few had mobile phones out and were recording.

It looked as if there was a large tear from the sky, right down to the ground near their feet. Part of the shop next door was just gone, a jagged edge left, with some bricks still falling.

Inside the tear, seemed to be empty space. It was a vague grey colour. A car had been unable to stop in time as the rip appeared, and was now stopped, the back half on the road, the front half, with the driver, just non-existent.

"Orsinius," Adriana said quietly, "Is this what the border between reality and unreality looks like?"

"No," Orsinius answered. "I have never seen anything like this before."

Out of the greyness, there was a movement. A thing appeared, it was at least three metres high and a metre and a half wide. It was vaguely human-shaped, but appeared to be made out of black rocks.

"Do you think this is what you have those things for?" Adriana asked, but no-one heard her question.

Orsinius had already entered the Interim, the time between the tick and the tock, and was outside of time. To him, everything was frozen in time as he ran, faster than he ever had before, to his burrow.

Rushing past mountains of hoarded stolen items, from shopping lists, to biros, to the crown jewels of a small country, he went to the deepest part of the burrow. There, among his most precious possessions, he collected the two mythical items Merlin had trusted to his care. Excalibur oozed the strongest magic he'd encountered, the Grail, something like, but not quite the same as, magic, which smelled even stronger.

Orsinius re-entered time in the same place he had left it. He handed the Grail to Ariana. "Fill this with coffee," he said.

"Coffee?" she asked, incredulous. Orsinius was already gone, so she went and did as he said, returning with the full cup.

In the meantime, Orsinius, brandishing Excalibur clumsily, rushed at the giant rock creature.

It was the strength of the magical object, rather than any skill on the wisp's part, that drove the monster back inside the rip.

"The cup!" Orsinius called to Ariana.

She handed him the Grail. He swirled the coffee in the cup then splashed it out over the rip, that sealed up again instantly.

The road was back. The next-door shop was back. The car was back, but damaged, and there was no sign of the driver.

"You did it." Ariana gasped. Then she asked, "Why coffee."

Orsinius, his heart still beating so hard he thought it was going to explode, answered, "It is a magic liquid. I thought it could carry some of the not-quite-magic in the Grail. I am surprised it worked."

"Oh," said Ariana, not at all certain that the explanation made sense. "Now what? All these people saw what happened? Isn't magic some kind of secret?"

"I think..." Orsinius thought about his answer. "I think, we have done enough. I think someone smarter than me, someone like Merlin, can deal with that. I think I want to have my coffee now."

"About that: I figured you needed coffee in the Grail quickly. I didn't make any, I just threw ours in there. How about we just lock up and go out for coffee?"

A Warning of Things to Come

Only six months ago, I didn't even know the magical world existed. Then my sister used magic against me, and a weird little bald man, with a long beard, and big ears, came to my rescue.

Now Orsinius Wishlet, a wisp, works in my hairdressing salon, making appointments, sweeping up hair and making coffee. He's my friend, as well as my rescuer. I've met numerous magical beings, many of them have become my customers. Apparently, it's hard to find someone to cut your hair if you're covering up things like wings that can get in the way.

Yesterday, something seemed to try to tear a hole in our world, and Orsinius fought it back with the help of Excalibur and coffee which he'd had me put into the Holy Grail.

I don't understand what all that was about, and neither does Orsinius. He had Excalibur and the Grail because Merlin, the mythical magician from King Arthur's court, had asked him to look after them.

Orsinius and I are meeting Merlin at the Bouncing Bean coffee shop, here in Lilly Pilly Lane, near the salon. We both want answers, and hopefully he has them.

We're here first. Merlin walks in. Most of the magical beings I have met try to fit in. They dress the same way as humans, and use a magical glamour to disguise any obvious differences such as wings or extra eyes or tails. Merlin just looks like what he is. He dresses as he probably did in King Arthur's court, with the pointed hat, and robes and the wooden staff. He looks like Gandalf.

People turn to look, then go back to their own coffees and conversations.

Merlin puts his hat and staff on the empty chair beside him. A waitress takes our orders. Once she's gone, he begins to talk. "It's all right Miss Sutton. People rationalise what they don't understand. Many of the people here think I'm on my way to or from a comic convention. The person behind you thinks I'm probably crazy but most likely harmless. The waitress thinks it's great that I'm confident to dress the way I want to, because she secretly wants to wear goth clothes to work but is afraid of people's reactions. Actually, her boss would be quite happy for her to wear whatever she wants because she's a very good employee."

I don't know how he knows what I'm thinking, but it's probably the same way he knows what everyone else is thinking.

"You wanted to know about the incident yesterday? You handled that very well, Mr Wishlet, with your very useful assistance, of course, Miss Sutton. Using a mild magical liquid like coffee to access the power of the cup was a brilliant plan. Mr Wishlet, do you know what is beyond Reality?"

"Yes," Orsinius answers. "It is Unreality. I have seen it. My burrow is on the border. But whatever that was yesterday was not Unreality."

"No, it was definitely not Unreality. Do you know what is beyond Unreality?"

"I have never thought about it," Orsinius answers.

"Well, I can tell you," Merlin answers. "Beyond Unreality are multiple other Realities. Unreality is the buffer that stops different Realities colliding. The event you stopped was a tear between our Reality and another."

"But," I ask, "if Realities can't collide because of Unreality, how did this happen?" Any time before six months ago, I would have never imagined myself saying the kinds of things I say now, especially not something like this.

We stop talking as the waitress arrives with our coffees and food. I notice the particular smile she gives Merlin. I hope she is brave enough to dress the way she wants for work tomorrow.

Once she leaves, Merlin answers my question. "It should not be possible, Miss Sutton," he says. "But something very strange is happening at the moment. There have been shifts in Reality. You, in fact, have been a part of it, although unknowingly. That spell your sister used against you should not have worked. Lady Justice found the actual spell. It was just nonsensical words, with no power behind them at all. Yet it worked, and you were trapped until Mr Wishlet found you. Things that cannot happen, that defy the laws of magic are happening."

"How can that be?" Orsinius asks.

"We believe, that is Lady Justice and I believe, that there is a magical practitioner breaking the rules of magic. We don't know what this person is trying to do, or whether or not they are achieving their goal, but they are using forms of magic which are banned. These forms of magic are so dangerous that they create an effect that send ripples out into the world, the way a rock thrown in a still pond sends out ripples. These ripples have had a number of effects on both the magical and non magical worlds. So a nonsense spell from a novelty book actually worked, realities that should never meet have broken in on each other, and I am afraid of what might happen next. But, for reasons I do not understand, the two of you seem to be at the centre of these events. In fact, Miss Sutton, you specifically are at the centre of the events as Mr Wishlet only happened to be there to discover you trapped. So perhaps the ripple only went in one direction, not across the whole pond."

"I'm the centre of events?" I ask, incredulous. "Why me? Why would magical side effects target me?"

"My thought would be that you have some relationship to the practitioner involved. Strong magic requires a price to be paid. I don't mean mild magic like coffee, or my casual mind reading earlier. Magic aimed at having a big effect, has a cost. Usually that price is taken close to home."

"But I didn't even know the magical world existed until that day my sister did that spell, and Orsinius found me! How would I have any links to any magical practitioner?"

"The nonsense spell your sister used came from an old book. Could that book have come from someone in your family?"

"Maybe my grandmother? I never met her, but my mother said she was crazy and thought she was a witch and could make things happen, but of course she actually couldn't."

"That information could be helpful. Lady Justice and I will continue our research, and we will definitely look into your ancestors. Perhaps your grandmother's belief was based in something that was far more real than your mother knew. In the meantime, I want you to wear this amulet, for protection. Mr Wishlet, as the guardian of Excalibur you already have the best magical protection available."

I put on the gold chain. It has a gold disc with what looks like a giant ruby in the middle. It feels warm against my skin.

I don't really want to know what it's going to protect me from.

Witch

Ariana Sutton and her friend and employee Orsinius Wishlet had coffee together most mornings before opening Ariana's hair salon.

This morning Ariana told her friend about a strange experience of the night before.

"I dreamed, well I think it was a dream, about a strange old woman being in my room, telling me something about a family heritage, but I don't clearly remember what she was saying. When I woke up, or maybe I didn't wake up and it was still a dream, I saw a witch on a broomstick flying outside the window. Is that crazy or what?"

Orsinius shrugged his shoulders. "Dreams are strange. Everything dreams, humans, animals, even wisps and other magical beings. Some people think dreams tell the future, but others say they are our minds' way of working things out. I do not know. Perhaps Merlin could tell you what it might mean." Orsinius was surprised that he could say the name of the great magician so casually, as if the great Merlin was a friend. At one time, even the name of Merlin would have struck him with fear and awe. These past few months had been very strange indeed.

"Whatever it was, it was a strange dream." Ariana finished her coffee and rinsed her mug out in the break room sink.

Her first two clients of the day arrived as she was unlocking the front door.

Lady Justice and her teenaged daughter Andromeda entered. Andromeda sat in the stylist's chair while Lady Justice sat in the waiting area.

"Good morning," Ariana said in her cheery working voice. "Andy, I'm just going to have to feel for your wings, behind the glamour, so I know where they are and don't accidentally cut you." Prior to her disastrous wedding, Ariana would never have imagined herself uttering such a sentence. Now this was a normal day's work.

"I don't care if you cut them," Andy said sadly. "I hate my wings. I hate being different."

"I guess when you've spent your whole life thinking you are a human girl, finding out you are something different, and especially growing wings, must have been a terrible shock," Ariana said, feeling a great sympathy for a girl who had also only recently been introduced to this strange world.

"On that topic," Lady Justice said from the waiting area chair, "I have some news for you, which you might find disturbing. Perhaps we could talk after you've done our hair, if you have time."

With no-one booked for the appointment immediately after these two, Ariana agreed.

Over coffee in the break room, Lady Justice asked: "What do you know about witches?"

"You mean Wiccans or…"

"I mean the type people tried to hunt, hang or burn, although the real witches rarely allowed themselves to be recognised or caught. I mean the type with real power."

"I guess I don't know anything about them, really."

"You said your grandmother thought she was a witch, and your sister cast a nonsense spell that shouldn't have worked, but it did. That was enough for me, with Merlin's assistance, to look into your family history. There have been a number of witches in your family line, although you might not have realised it. One of them, your grandmother's aunt was especially famous. In fact, the author Bram Stoker wrote a novel about her."

"Bram Stoker? Wasn't he the person who wrote Dracula?"

"He also wrote a book called The Lair of the White Worm, about a witch named Lady Arabella March. Have you read it?"

Ariana shook her head again, "No, I haven't read it."

"You might want to. Lady Arabella March was your grandmother's aunt. It's no wonder your grandmother thought she was a witch, she believed she could be the same as her aunt. However this power is dormant in some people, it doesn't appear in every generation of a family. Your sister clearly did have it. Given recent occurrences, Merlin and I believe you may as well. It may well be an innate talent which you have not been aware of, because you have never tried to use it."

"You think I'm a witch?"

"I think it's entirely possible."

"If I'm a witch, could my dreams foretell the future or something?"

"Perhaps. Have you had a dream that particularly concerns you?"

Ariana retold the story she'd told Orsinius that morning.

Lady Justice listened carefully. "According to Stoker's book, Arabella March died, but there are widespread rumours that she cheated death and lives on. She was, perhaps still is, a very dangerous woman. I find your dream very disturbing, if it was a dream. It may be that you are a witch, unknowingly, and your dream was more than a dream. If you are willing, I would like to suggest that you work with Merlin, to learn the extent of your abilities, if you have any, and to learn how to use them to protect yourself and possibly others. Orsinius, if anything should happen and you or Miss Sutton, if you require my assistance, I want you to use the Interim to come for me. Don't rely on human communications systems because they are too slow. I know you are adjusting to the human world, but remember who you are and what your skills are."

Orsinius bowed low. "Your Ladyship, I will never forget how our world works, no matter how much time I spend among humans."

After Lady Justice and Andromeda left, Ariana looked at Orsinius, not knowing what to say. He shrugged his shoulders.

"Am I really a witch?" Ariana asked. "What does that even mean?"

"I do not know." Orsinius said. "I have not met witches. Even in the magical world, real witches are rare. I do know you are a good person, so if you are a witch, you are a good witch."

"Thanks," Ariana said. "Now, I have to work out how to use magic, and how to avoid a possibly not dead great great whatever aunt, who wants who knows what from me. Things were easier before."

Orsinius thought back to his days as a simple thief. "Things were indeed easier before," he said.

Perspective

Orsinius Wishlet sat in his burrow on the border between reality and unreality.

His time among humans had given him a new perspective on his collection. He now knew that his previously treasured collection of pieces of paper: old shopping lists, cash register dockets, bills, scrap paper from long-forgotten notepads, was actually rubbish.

The pens and biros in his collection had a purpose, but he had so many of them they would never be able to use them all.

His odd socks, and other knitted and fabric items represented an inconvenience to the humans he had stolen them from, but had no further value. He had learned that socks needed to be in a pair to be of practical use.

Much of his jewellery collection was cheap junk that the humans he had stolen it from would not care about the loss. His more prized jewellery, and the artworks stolen from museums, were valuable to the humans he had stolen them from, but only gave him a sense of guilt. He considered returning it all, but he had stolen so much in his time as a thief he had no idea where his treasures belonged.

He considered throwing out the rubbish items, but his cousin Augustus had already entered the burrow in his absence to steal his true treasures. He needed the rubbish to trick any thief who would steal from him, the former master thief, into thinking that all in his burrow was rubbish.

Carefully, he cleaned and polished the two real treasures the great wizard Merlin had trusted to his possession: the sword Excalibur, and the holy grail. He began with Excalibur.

Life had been strange for Orsinius in the past couple of months. His new friend and employer Ariana Sutton had been a big part of the change. Now he had learned that Ariana might actually unknowingly be a witch.

He had told her that because she was a good human, if she were a witch, she must be a good witch. Still, he was troubled. Even in his world, witches were extremely rare, and good witches were almost unheard of.

After Ariana had done so much to help him learn to live without stealing, he felt he had to help her learn to stay good once she began to use magic.

"Can it be possible that she is a witch and still stays good?" he asked quietly of the sword in his hand. Excalibur seemed to grow warm for a moment, and then returned to its normal cool temperature. "You say, yes?" The sword warmed then cooled again.

Orsinius turned his attention to cleaning and polishing the grail. He had used the magical fluid coffee to carry its power, and he did not want to leave coffee stains in such a precious object.

As he carefully polished a mountain of jewellery shifted slightly, then collapsed on top of him. Instead of crushing him, it formed an arch over him. Either the grail, or Excalibur or both prevented anything actually landing on him. He was cocooned in the collapsed finery, but had a small safe bubble around him.

What could he do now? He yelled for help. There should not have been anyone but him in the burrow, so he knew it was pointless, but he yelled anyway. He yelled several more times.

Then he heard it. It was a scraping and a clattering, and a frantic crashing.

Eventually one side of his wall of shiny things opened, and there was Ariana throwing things aside madly.

"Orsinius, are you all right?" she asked.

He grabbed the grail and the sword and dived out from under the mountain of jewels, as it all crashed into the space where his bubble of safety had been.

He looked at his friend in wonder. "How are you here?" he asked. "Humans cannot be here, not on the border. Humans can only live in reality."

"I don't know." She sounded confused. "One minute I was home watching tv, then I heard you call and the next moment I was here, and I knew you needed me to clear away all this stuff. Where is here? Is this your burrow?"

"This is my burrow. This is the border between Reality and Unreality. This is a place humans cannot survive, but you are here. It is true. You are a witch."

"I'm a witch. When Lady Justice said that might be a possibility I didn't really believe it. Now I don't know what to believe. I am here, and I shouldn't be. I don't know how I got here, or how I can get back where I belong."

"The only way back I know is through the Interim."

Ariana shuddered. She'd been trapped in the Interim when she'd first met Orsinius, as a result of a spell her sister had cast.

"I don't think that's how I got here. In the Interim, everything else stood still, but I moved. I would have noticed moving through a world staying still. It was instant. I mean it was instant for me, if you understand what I mean. Besides, we needed Lady Justice to get me out of the Interim before. I don't think I would have known how to get back into it to use it to move from one place to another."

"I think you will learn this. I think now we know you have power, I can teach you. You taught me how to live without stealing. I will teach you how to live with magic."

Andy

Mum said keeping a diary might help me adjust to all the changes. I'm giving it a go, but it's all just so much.

Two weeks ago, I just had normal grade eleven girl problems. Could I juggle Debating practice with Netball training, with my Ancient History and English assignments? Would I be the only girl to get through high school without ever having a boyfriend? Would other kids stop picking on me for being named Andromeda? Would I always feel left out, as if I didn't belong?

Well I know the answer to that last one now. I don't belong.

The day after my sixteenth birthday, I woke up with horrible pains in my back. Mum called the school and said I was sick and couldn't go to school that day or the next. Then she made me my favourite breakfast, pancakes, and told me the truth.

I'm not human. The pain in my back was my wings beginning to grow.

My mother's not just an ordinary lawyer, like I'd always thought. She's Lady Justice, the arbiter of all magical justice, and I'm going to be the next Lady Justice. My mother's over five hundred years old and got her wings when she was sixteen. She says it's always been like that.

She also tells me that every Lady Justice has a daughter when she's five hundred, and then only lives another hundred years to train her daughter to take over.

For years I've been asking about my father, and my mother's refused to tell me anything about him. Now she tells me I don't have a father, and my daughter, who I have when I'm five hundred won't have a father either.

She's taught me how to do a "glamour", magic to make my wings invisible to humans. The whole magical world is some

44

kind of big secret. I can't tell any of my school friends. So yeah, if I felt like I didn't belong before, I feel even more like I don't belong now.

There was one human who knew about the secret. She'd stumbled into it and there was no point hiding it from her. Her name's Ariana. She's my hairdresser. Just a couple of days ago, my mother and Merlin (Mum's friends with Merlin, yes that Merlin) explained to her that she's actually some magical creature as well. She's some kind of witch from an ancient line of powerful witches. In among her family was a witch so evil the guy who wrote Dracula also wrote a book about her. (I wonder if that means Dracula is real as well? I should ask Mum.) So I guess Ariana knows what I'm going through.

My mother says she thought it was important to give me time to be a normal kid. Her mother told her who and what she was right from when she was little, and she never had anything to do with humans for years. She says me growing up as human lets me learn about that world, and now I have to learn about my own world (the magical world) as well. She says the two cross over more than I think.

I wanted to go to uni. I wanted to get a normal job and do normal things. Mum says I can still do all of that. She says I've got till I'm a hundred before I have to take over from her. I can have a human lifetime, as long as I learn from her as well, and then go on and do my "real" job when she dies.

But what if I don't want to be the next "Lady Justice"? My mother says no-one in the family line has ever refused. She says the whole magical world and the non-magical world, depend on someone ensuring that no-one misuses magic. She says I will accept my "responsibility" by the time I'm a hundred.

I want to go back to the day before my birthday, when I was still just another teenager who tried too hard and still didn't fit in.

A Strange Request

The tall, gaunt woman in the long black dress swept through the quiet outer Brisbane street.

She smiled slightly on overhearing a youthful voice say, "Boomer goth." The teenager had no idea of who or what she was.

Entering the nondescript bookshop, the woman ignored the bored cashier and walked purposefully to the back wall of the shop. There she slid the final bookshelf aside, walked through and closed the door behind her.

In the real shop now, she was surrounded by strange objects. Foetuses of various animals, including human, floated in formaldehyde in jars. Herbs and spices, some mundane, some exotic, some toxic, were clearly labelled in jars on shelves either side of a curtain behind the counter. Medallions of occult symbols, made from a variety of metals occupied a glass cabinet beneath the counter. Vials of blood, venom and other liquids were in a small refrigerator to the side of the shop. Crows in cages and giant spiders in glass boxes were on shelves against the opposite wall. The whole shop was cluttered, dark and had the vile smell of damp.

A black cat, which had been lying lazily on the counter, jumped up onto all four paws, legs straight, back arched, tail upright, and hissed before darting to a hiding place in a dark corner.

The woman looked disdainfully at a mummified monkey's paw. Then she turned her attention to the weaselly-looking wisp, with a bald head and long grey beard, perched on a stool behind the counter.

"You are Augustus Wishlet." It was a statement, not a question.

"I am," he replied. He noticed her walking stick more than her. It was a black wooden stick, with a handle formed of a silver snake's head. The snake had green stones, possibly emeralds, as eyes, and its tail wound round the length of the stick.

"Lady Arabella March. You've heard of me." Again it was a statement. Bram Stoker had ensured the whole world had heard of her. Stoker hadn't been entirely truthful, particularly with respect to her death, but had ensured she was always shown the utmost respect, if not outright fear. She had moved from England to Australia to avoid some of the notoriety. It had made sense of a kind as all her problems had begun with a man moving from Australia to England. Disappointingly, she found Stoker's book had preceded her.

Augustus nodded, sweat beads forming on his bald head. "How may I help you, Lady Arabella?" He tried to sound casual, but polite. This was not a person he wanted to risk offending in any way.

"I'm told you can get absolutely anything, no matter how obscure."

"Oh yes, I do have that reputation, and so far no-one has given me a request I could not fulfil." The emerald eyes seemed to glint at him.

"I need the head of a hanged man. A bare skull will do." She said it as casually as if asking the greengrocer for a head of cabbage.

Did that snake head move?

"That is not an easy request to fulfil. There have not been any hangings in Australia since the late nineteen sixties. I suppose it is possible to rob a grave, but it would take a significant amount of research to find the right one, and it would not be easy to find someone to undertake the job. Then of course, there is the matter of decomposition and whether the skull would still be intact after so many years." He sounded doubtful, but was also clearly terrified.

"This is very disappointing. I was informed you could get anything."

"Well, it is a strange request. I am sure I can acquire an appropriate skull, but it may take some time, and quite a bit of money. I would have to find and hire the right person, and for that person to find and exhume the right body. People with that particular skillset are rare, and they charge a great deal."

That snake absolutely did move. He was sure of it.

"Money is not an issue, but time most definitely is. I require it before the next full moon."

"I cannot guarantee that is possible." Emerald eyes seemed to glare malevolently.

"There's an easier, most likely faster, alternative," Arabella said thoughtfully. "There is a famous skull that has been in private circulation since the nineteen seventies. You could persuade the current owner to sell."

"You want Ned's head?" the small man gasped.

"Ned's head would do the job nicely," she replied. "He was definitely hanged, and definitely deserved it. Yes, Ned would be perfect for my purposes. Do you know who has it?"

The head of the snake was no longer on the top of the walking stick, but had moved up on to Arabella's hand. Its eyes glinted at Augustus menacingly.

He gulped, still staring at the snake rather than at the woman who was looking down on him. "The collector who has it, is very wealthy, and very attached to the skull. He will not give it up for any price."

"Well, then," she said, "you must use your other skills to acquire it."

"Impossible," he said. "This man's security is state of the art, and, well, he is known to be a practitioner with even greater powers than yours. If I attempted to steal the skull, I would be just as dead as Ned himself. I am afraid that Ned's head is the first request that I cannot fulfil."

The snake's head was now on the counter, with its tail following around the stick and over the customer's hand. The emerald eyes started, menacing and unblinking, at the shopkeeper.

"You are sure you cannot acquire this object for me?"

The snake slithered its way across the counter and was starting its way up the wisp's arm.,

Quivering in fear, pouring sweat and unable to look away from the dark green eyes, he answered quietly, "I'm am not able to."

"Then give me the name of the person who currently possesses it." Her voice seemed to float into his mind from a great distance, while the snake reared up, and looked at him face to face, only centimetres apart.

Augustus, transfixed, said quietly. "I can't tell you his name, if he found out, he would kill me."

"Tell me, or I will kill you myself," she answered, "or I will have Worm do it. She has clearly developed an interest in you."

"I cannot tell you his name. He would know and he would kill me. But you know him already. Everyone knows him. He is very rich and very famous. You must have seen his yellow billboards everywhere."

She nodded. "Worm, we're leaving."

The snake instantly returned to its place on the walking stick, and was perfectly still, as if Augustus had only imagined it moving. Lady Arabella turned to leave.

"Oh Lady Arabella," a suddenly much braver Augustus said to her back. "There is a fee for information here."

She turned to look back at him. "What information?" she asked. "You said yourself you were unable to give me his name.

She opened the bookshelf door and left.

Augustus took a large handkerchief from his trousers pocket and patted down his sweaty head. He went to the bookshelf door and locked it, checking to be sure it was secure.

He drew aside the heavy black velvet curtain behind the counter, revealing the door to a large room-sized safe. He opened the door and entered. In the safe were his most valuable possessions. In the centre of the room was a pedestal, topped with a glass box that contained an old, very worn, human skull. At the back of the skull a chunk of bone was missing, having been removed during the autopsy after the hanging. Most of the teeth were missing, having been taken by souvenir hunters years before.

Beside the pedestal, was an old worn leather armchair. Augustus sat. The cat, having emerged from his hiding place leapt into Augustus' lap. The cat knew that this was their routine at the end of the day, and he curled himself into a silky fur donut to purr and be stroked, as his master went through his afternoon ritual of conversing with the skull.

"That was close, Ned," Augustus said. "Honestly, I was so scared for a moment there that I almost handed you over to her. But you and I, we are so much alike. We are both thieves, out of necessity and neither of us want to kowtow to people like her, people who think money and power put them in charge of us. I could not give you to that monster. I could not ever do that to you."

Augustus thought a moment, and smiled smugly. "Can I tell you a secret? I might have lied a little bit. Well, actually I might have lied a lot. I do not like rich people who think they own everything and everyone. You understand that, do you not? Of course you do. So now, there is a billionaire who is about to receive the surprise of his life. Oh that old witch woman will come back here furious when she finds out he is not what I said and he does not have you, but we will cross that bridge when we come to it, will we not? By then, we will have thought of something."

Just as it was every other afternoon, this was an entirely one-sided conversation. Ned, whose real humanity had been irretrievably lost to folklore and whose skull had been lost and then found at least twice before Augustus had finally acquired it, was unable to speak. Augustus, however, was absolutely certain he could feel a response: that the hanged man agreed with him entirely, and was glad to be safe in his care.

Trouble

Orsinius Wishlet was at home in his burrow on the border between reality and unreality. It was cluttered with all of the many things he had stolen and hoarded in his long time as a thief.

Now that he spent so much time among humans Orsinius knew that many of the things, such as old shopping lists and odd socks were really not treasures at all, although they had seemed so attractive to him long ago. He kept the items anyway, so it was more difficult for thieves to enter his burrow and steal the things of real value he had been tasked with protecting.

While the border between Reality and Unreality where his burrow was placed was inaccessible to humans, it was only too accessible to other magical beings, such his cousin Augustus, who was a non-reformed thief.

With the help of his friend Ariana, Orsinius had developed a doorbell, or burglar alarm, of sorts. Anyone entering the mouth of the burrow now would have to pass through hanging strings of cans, pans, and any other hard objects they'd been able to find in his collection that would clang together noisily. If Orsinius was in the burrow, he would hear the noise.

Ariana had used the magic she'd recently learned to provide a second layer of protection. If Orsinius was away from the burrow he would hear in his mind the clanging of the "doorbell". She had not been happy about using magic on his mind, but he had persuaded her that it was necessary, given the importance of the items hidden in the deepest part of the burrow.

While Orsinius and Ariana were enjoying coffee after finishing the day's work in Ariana's hair salon, the sudden clanging filled Orsinius' mind.

Ariana saw the startled expression on her friend's face, and knew what it meant. "I'm coming too," she said.

Ordinarily, Orsinius would use the Interim, that time between moments, to go quickly from the salon, firmly in reality, to the burrow, on the border with unreality. Ariana had another way. She grabbed Orsinius' arm, and thought them there.

"Augustus!" Orsinius yelled. "You are here to steal again?"

Augustus threw himself at Orsinius' feet. "I am not here to steal. I am here with my most prized possession, to ask you to protect me. You have Excalibur. You can keep me safe."

They saw Augustus had with him, a black wooden box, and a cat carrier with a black cat in it.

Orsinius introduced Augustus to Ariana.

"A witch?" Augustus asked, and tried to shrink into the wall of the burrow.

Eventually Augustus was calm enough to tell them his story. He had been visited in his shop by a powerful witch, who had wanted to buy his most precious possession. He had tricked her into leaving, but knew she would be back and would kill him. Augustus carefully avoided mentioning that the witch had a silver snake on her walking stick which was actually alive. He would not tell them what the possession in the box was.

They listened attentively to his story. Then he told them the name of the witch: Lady Arabella March.

"I'm getting Lady Justice, and Merlin," Ariana said.

"No! Not Lady Justice. I did not do anything wrong!"

Ariana disappeared. Moments later she was back with Lady Justice and Merlin.

"I did nothing wrong!" Augustus wailed, grovelling in front of the newcomers.

"What exactly was this thing Lady Arabella wanted from you?" Merlin asked, gently. "It's very important, for you to tell us, so we can protect you."

Augustus sniffed, and opened the box. Inside was a human skull, battered and old.

"Is this anyone in particular? Anything about this person's life or death which was special?" Merlin asked.

"He was a thief, a great thief." Augustus said sadly, "and he was hanged."

Merlin nodded, then asked, "Did she say what she needed it for? Or that she needed it by a set time?"

"She did not say what she needed it for. She did say she wanted it before the next full moon."

Merlin thought a few moments, then said, "I believe she is making a spell designed to steal powers from another witch. Miss Sutton, I very much expect that witch would be you. The familial link would make it easier to steal power from you. Indeed, we have a serious issue here. In the few lessons we have had together so far, I have seen your power and potential. That power added to the power of someone like Lady Arabella, and used for evil purposes, could be extremely dangerous. She already opened up a rift between realities, which Mr Orsinius Wishlet, with your capable assistance, was able to stop. She could do so much worse with your incredible power added to hers."

He stopped to think some more, then addressed Augustus. "I don't suppose you would be willing to allow me to destroy Mr Kelly's skull, would you Mr Wishlet?"

Augustus gulped. How had the information he'd given been enough for Merlin to know who the skull was? "It is my favourite possession, and … and my only friend." Augustus said.

"I see you have another friend with you as well," Merlin said, looking into the cat carrier. Yellow cat eyes glared back.

"I must recommend you and both your friends stay here. This is as defensible position as we are going to get. Mr Wishlet, other Mr Wishlet, I am afraid you are having a number of houseguests. Lady Justice, Miss Sutton and I must stay here to help protect your cousin and his most prized possession from Lady Arabella. I believe we may need to have Excalibur ready, along with the grail."

Lady Justice said, "If we are staying, I will need to bring Andy here. I can't leave her alone at home with this danger about."

Lady Justice went home to get her teenaged daughter.

Andy was not there. Instead there was a note which said: "You want your daughter. I want the skull. Meet me at Augustus Wishlet's shop at midnight tonight."

Ransom

Giving in to a criminal is not how I normally do things, but my daughter's life is on the line, and Merlin has a plan.

I try not to look at the products on the shelves. Augustus Wishlet's shop is disturbing enough during the day. At night it's even worse.

I have the black box Augustus was carrying the skull in.

Tucked out of sight, under my left wing, is my sword. I can have it in my hand instantly if things do not go to plan, although Merlin tells me it would be useless. At her full strength, this witch would kill me before I could swing the sword.

The witch has appeared, with Andy. Andy's wrist is tied to hers with what appears to be a silver ornamental snake with green, possibly emerald eyes.

They didn't step out of the Interim, the time between moments most magical beings use to move from place to place. They just appeared. Lady Arabella March uses the same thought magic as Ariana uses.

"The skull," she says.

I hold up the box. "Andy first," I answer.

The snake slowly uncoils from Andy's wrist. I put the box on the shop counter and step back. She keeps a hand on Andy's arm as she walks to the counter, and looks in the box. In the box she sees the battered old skull which means so much to Augustus.

She releases Andy. I grab Andy's wrist and drag her into the Interim.

Instead of moving through the Interim, we are suddenly in Orsinius Wishlet's burrow on the border between reality and unreality.

"I saw Lady Arabella was about to follow you through the Interim," Merlin says. "So I asked Miss Sutton to bring you here her way."

Ariana looks strained. She used a lot of energy to bring us here, and is still concentrating on the glamour, a kind of glamour I have never seen before, strong enough to let a witch like Lady Arabella see a skull when she's actually presented with a basketball. It's only a matter of time, before Ariana has to break concentration, and the deception will be revealed.

In the meantime, Merlin is directing the rest of his plan, moving people and props.

Andy is sent to the very depths of the burrow with Augustus and his cat. Augustus is taking the skull with him.

I am near the mouth of the burrow. My sword is no longer hidden.

Orsinius is holding Excalibur. Merlin says only a magical sword like Excalibur could possibly kill the snake. The snake holds a part of Arabella March's power. Destroying it is Orsinius' job. Only months ago, Orsinius was a petty thief, and an annoyance. Now he's helping fight for the safety of the world.

Merlin is having Ariana drink coffee, out of the Grail. In solving a problem caused by Lady Arabella, Orsinius and Ariana had discovered that the mild magical properties of coffee could act as a carrier for the power of the Grail. The Grail is not magical itself, as we know magic, but has its own, different kind of power. Merlin says it's touched by divinity.

The coffee seems to restore Ariana's strength. This is good, because we will be relying on Ariana. It is her power Lady Arabella is coming to steal, and her power that must stand against her. Merlin will add his magic to hers.

For now, Merlin is organising us, while watching Lady Arabella. He was able to find her, by knowing where she would be for the kidnapping ransom. Once he found her, he's been able to follow.

My part in all of this, is the part I always play. Lady Justice will render ultimate justice.

"She is ready to begin her spell," Merlin says. "Miss Sutton, you can let go now."

Ariana exhales slowly. Then everything happens at once.

Lady Arabella is here, screeching. The snake is reared up, its tail around her walking stick, its head waving in the air. The emerald eyes are locked on to Ariana.

The snake's eyes are glowing green and are sending twin beams of green light at Ariana. A protective amulet with a ruby centre that Ariana is wearing is sending a larger, red beam back at the snake, over whelming the green beams.

Ariana steps forward, ignoring the snake, and is staring fixedly at Lady Arabella.

Lady Arabella, is now staring straight back at Ariana, eyes locked, neither blinking.

With both the snake and Lady Arabella staring fixedly at Ariana, neither notice Orsinius, as he swings Excalibur. The snake's head is removed from its body. It quivers a moment, and stops. It is simply a broken silver decoration.

Lady Arabella shudders. She is weakened by the loss of her familiar. She pulls herself up straight, seems more determined.

Merlin is standing behind Ariana, his hand on her right shoulder. Both Merlin and Ariana seem weakened. Lady Arabella appears to be gaining strength.

Out of nowhere, Augustus' cat comes running, leaps up on to Ariana's left shoulder, and glares at Lady Arabella. Its yellow eyes seem to glow.

The power seems to shift again, Ariana is stronger. Lady Arabella is on her knees.

"She's weak enough. Time for the Sword of Justice," Merlin says.

I swing my ancestral sword as I have done so many times before. In one smooth movement, her head is removed from her body. Lady Arabella March will never misuse magic again.

Ariana collapses on the floor. The cat snuggles in beside her. Merlin is bent over, shaking. "Coffee," he says. "We need coffee, Even for the cat."

Aftermath

It is a strange group of beings who are gathered in the burrow on the border between reality and unreality.

There is Orsinius Wishlet, a wisp, short and bald with over-large pointed ears. He is a reformed kleptomaniac, and a hoarder, and this burrow, his home, is cluttered with the remnants of his past life. He is the current guardian of both Excalibur and the Holy Grail.

Augustus Wishlet is Orsinius' cousin. He is an unreformed thief, who looks similar to his cousin, and works as a purveyor of arcane, disgusting, and hard-to-find objects. With him is his most prized possession, a battered bare skull of a long-ago hanged thief.

Lady Justice is a strong statuesque woman with a five metre wing span, who has with her a razor-sharp ancestral sword. By right of inheriting the position she is the final arbiter of all law in the magical world. Her judgment is swift, and offenders do not have the opportunity to appeal or to reoffend.

Andromeda Justice (Andy to her friends) is the teenaged daughter of Lady Justice. Her wings have just started to grow. She has spent her life thinking she was human, and has only recently learned the truth of who she is, and her destiny to inherit her mother's role.

There is the ancient wizard Merlin. He is the only member of the group not wearing modern human clothes. He has flowing robes, a pointed wizard's hat, and a long wooden staff with translucent gemstone set into it. If one watches, the gemstone changes colour, and there are swirls within it. He has a long white beard, and flowing white hair. He looks like Gandalf.

A black cat with glowing yellow eyes, is alternately preening itself, and pawing at a broken silver snake with emerald eyes.

The final, living, person in the burrow is Ariana Sutton. Like Andy, she had until recently, believed she was human. To her, it seems as if it were only yesterday that other members of the group explained to her that she was, in fact, a powerful witch. Merlin has undertaken to be her teacher, although her magic is not like his. She uses thought magic, the rarest kind of magic. Her thoughts can create reality.

On the floor is the rapidly withering and disintegrating body of one of Ariana's ancestors, the infamous witch Lady Arabella March. Lady Arabella had survived an unnatural length of time by use of the same thought magic her descendant now uses, supplemented with the use of spells. Her undoing had been a spell to steal Ariana's magic, to make herself the most powerful witch in history. The spell has been thwarted by the living members of the group, who substituted one of her ingredients.

The living watch the dead witch disintegrate to a fine dust. Merlin points his staff at the dust and it flies out of the burrow entrance to be dispersed along the border of reality and unreality.

Then Merlin breaks the silence, his voice quiet, gentle, as to a child. "Miss Sutton, in that final battle, as you overpowered Lady Arabella, her spell reversed itself. You felt it did you not?"

Ariana nods. She did feel it. She still does feel it. She doesn't think she will ever feel normal again.

"You have her power, added to your own considerable power," Merlin goes on. "If the spell had not reversed itself, you would likely have inherited her power anyway. Added to that, I believe Lady Justice will discover that you are now Lady Arabella's only living relative and will therefore inherit her not inconsiderable fortune in the human world."

61

Ariana nods slowly again, not certain she has really processed anything which has happened, still not sure of the immense power she feels flowing through her.

"You have undergone great changes in power and wealth. You must decide what you will do now," Merlin says.

There is a long pause.

"I'm going to go back to my hair salon, and cut my customer's hair," she finally answers. "I hope Orsinius will come with me and continue to be my assistant."

Orsinius smiles. This is all he hopes for. "Yes, I will continue to work with my friend," he says.

The cat wraps itself around her ankle, purring.

"If Augustus is willing, I would like to buy the cat," Ariana says.

Augustus looks at the cat. Until today it has been his, and it has not displayed any magical ability. During the fight, while he and Andy hid, the cat came forward to fight alongside Ariana and Merlin. He is frightened of the cat now he knows it has this power. This is definitely not a cat he wants to live with any longer. He does something he has never done in his life. He decides to give something away.

"The cat is yours," Augustus says. "It is choosing you." He secretly hopes this magnanimous gesture might buy him the favour of this powerful witch. He does not like powerful beings angry at him, but they often are.

"What's its name?" Ariana asks.

"I do not know," Augustus answers. "It came to me in the shop one day and did not leave. It did not tell me a name. I have simply called it 'the cat.'"

In Ariana's mind, 'the cat' deserved capitalisation at least. It became "The Cat."

On the south side of Brisbane, not far from the Brisbane River, in a boutique shopping district known as Lilly Pilly Lane, there is a small hairdressing salon. There a young hairdresser runs her business with the help of her strange-looking friend. A black cat with glowing yellow eyes, sits on the counter and watches everything and everyone.

Some of her customers are ordinary human beings, who are unaware of any world except the one they live in. They come for fashionable hair styles and friendly service.

Some of her customers hide wings and things under a glamour. They know their hairdresser is the most powerful witch the world has ever known, and that the odd little assistant is guardian to both the mythic magic sword Excalibur, and the Holy Grail. Word travels quickly in the magical community and everyone knows the story.

These customers come to the salon confident of two things: they will receive a good haircut, and powerful people are protecting the world and the nature of reality itself.

Everyone who comes to the salon is offered a mildly magical liquid, known as coffee.

Nutshell

Primrose had never been brave before. But then, she'd never had to.

She was a nursery maid, not a soldier, nor a guard. Her work had been in the quietest part of the castle. In a way she was responsible for the kingdom's greatest treasure, but she'd never imagined any threat to the baby princess.

Queen Rose's Castle had always been well guarded, although there was no real risk of attack. Surely no-one would ever attack the Fairy Queen.

No-one would attack the Fairy Queen, until someone did.

Lord Rust had led a party of elves to overthrow the castle. One

The fighting was terrible. The castle guards and the Queen's soldiers had trained, but had never really fought an invader before.

Daisy had rushed into the nursery and told Primrose the castle had fallen and Lord Rust's men were coming for the baby. Then, instead of helping, Daisy had run away.

Primrose, for the first time ever, had been forced to decide on quick action, and to take a dangerous risk. She'd grabbed the baby, and a basket with everything else she was able to carry, and she had sneaked out through the servant's entrance. Then she had run, the baby and the basket being too heavy to fly with.

Hearing the sounds of pursuit, Primrose had no choice, but to drop the basket and fly with the baby.

Elves, unlike fairies, were stuck on ground level, so flight allowed her to evade the elves chasing her.

She'd hid in the trees for a while, watching the elves as they searched. Sadly, she saw them find the basket, with everything she'd been able to pack in the minutes available. There would be no chance to retrieve it.

From behind the leaves of a tall tree, she'd watched and begun to think about her situation.

She'd never had to rely on her own resources before. But there she was, with the tiny, helpless, future queen depending on her to know how to keep both of them safe.

As soon as the elves were gone from sight, and she could no longer hear them, Primrose held baby Princess Aster close to her as she flew, further and further than she had ever been before. Her wings ached. Her arms felt heavy.

When she could fly no more, she'd stopped in a tree, to rest. Princess Aster was restless. She needed food, but that was in the basket. Primrose was exhausted, but knew the baby would need to be fed soon. She held the baby tight and cried. Primrose was a nursery maid. No one had trained her to be a hero, to rescue a princess.

Then she heard the gentle hum of a bee gathering pollen. Forcing herself to fly once more, she followed the sound, then followed the bee back to the hive. At the entrance, she begged a tiny bit of honey. "This baby is the child of a queen," she said to the bees. "Surely your own queen will look kindly on her."

The queen of the bees did take pity on the child, and both Primrose and baby Aster were given honey, with a tiny bit of royal jelly for baby Aster.

Feeling a little refreshed, Primrose decided to continue flying. She had no plan on where to go, but she flew.

It was dark when she came across the human settlement.

Primrose suddenly had the most wonderful thought. She would take the princess and hide among the humans. Neither fairies nor elves would go anywhere near a human habitation if they had a choice. They would be safe from elves there, at least until she worked out what to do next.

One building seemed to call to her. She did not know why. Primrose crept through a slightly open window.

This place had a strong smell. If Primrose had known about hair dye, she would have recognised it. She carried the baby through a huge room with white tiles on the floor. Primrose had never imagined a room could be so big. The next room she found seemed to be a kitchen of sorts, bigger than any kitchen she'd ever seen. Beside that was a store room. It was huge.

Primrose saw that the gap between the lowest shelves and the floor was large enough for fairies to be in. This would be their temporary home.

Primrose searched the kitchen and the store room, looking for things they would need. In a bin in the kitchen was half a walnut shell. It was the perfect size, to be a bed for the baby princess. She found scraps of food.

A day before, she would never have considered human's scraps suitable for the princess, but now the only thing that mattered was that they were alive and safe.

Primrose wondered if the queen was safe, or even alive. She wondered if the elves were in control of the whole fairy world, and if Lord Rust's elves were still looking for her and Princess Aster. She wondered how she would know when it was safe to take Princess Aster home. What were the humans who frequented this place like? Could she and the baby avoid detection?

Those were all problems she would have to solve, her, a nursery maid who had never done anything important ever.

But for one night, with the future of the fairy world in a nutshell, and herself on a bed made out of a sponge she'd found on a shelf in the store room, she needed to sleep, to recover.

Dolls' House

I knew it was going to be a tough conversation, telling Mum I didn't want to go to university.

She'd always said learning law, the way humans did it, was a good background for someone who would one day have to take over managing justice for the whole magical world.

I pointed out that I would not have to take over as Lady Justice until I'm a hundred. At not-quite-seventeen, that left a lot of time to study that. Before I had all that responsibility, I just wanted an ordinary life for a little while longer.

Lucky for me, Ariana wanted more help at the hair salon, and she'd need someone who understood the nature of most of her customers.

So the three of us reached an agreement: I would stay at school right to the end of grade twelve, but could work after school and on holidays at the salon. If I liked it, and Ariana was happy with my work, she would give me an apprenticeship after I finished school.

I did have to promise my mother I would start reading through the records of our ancestors' work. Every Lady Justice builds her work on the work of her mother, her grandmother, her great-grandmother, all the way back for thousands of years. Some of those records were in strange languages I would have to learn.

That day, I was in the store room, refilling shampoo and conditioner bottles from the big stock bottles there. I saw a movement on the edge of my peripheral vision.

Ariana was in the main salon area, cutting a customer's hair. Orsinius was in the break room, making coffee for the customer. So no-one should have been there.

I turned to look more closely, and saw a tiny flitter of a glittery wing. There, hiding behind a big bottle of perming solution was a tiny person, about ten centimetres tall, with gossamer-fine, glittering, wings.

"A fairy!" I said, "I've never seen a fairy before. My name's Andromeda, people call me Andy. What's your name?"

She was cowering in a corner. "A human! Oh I've made a big mistake!"

"No, I'm not human." I shook the glamour off my wings. Unlike hers mine were large, wings with coloured feathers. "I'm the daughter of Lady Justice, I guess that makes me part of a species of two."

"Lady Justice? The Lady Justice who judges all the magical world? Oh, perhaps she could help me."

The fairy, whose name was Primrose, told me her story. The fairy queen's castle had been overthrown by an elf Lord, and she had fled, carrying the baby princess, who was even now hidden in the storeroom.

Ariana's customer had left, and she was having a rare break, so I told Primrose, we needed to talk to her.

"Fairies are real?" Ariana asked.

Ariana was the world's most powerful witch, but had only discovered the magical world less than a year before, as I had.

When Primrose had told her story, Ariana told me to get my mother and Orsinius to get Merlin.

We both entered the Interim to do as she instructed. Of course we all had mobile phones, but we never used them for anything important. Using the Interim, it was possible to leave and be back with the person we were getting at the same instant. While I was at home, to tell my mother, I had a thought of something that might make things easier for Primrose.

Once we were all back, Ariana looked at my old dolls' house I had brought. "That's a very pink dolls' house," she said.

I blushed. When I was little I'd wanted everything pink. Other colours hadn't existed for me then.

"It's definitely better than a walnut shell on the floor for a baby princess, but I think I can make it a little better," Ariana said.

She held the dolls' house, and closed her eyes a moment. "OK. There's power, water and plumbing." Ariana used thought magic, which was very powerful.

We put the dolls' house on a shelf in the store room. Then Ariana sent me out for supplies, baby nappies, bottles and formula, food, and clothes for both the baby and Primrose. When I brought them back, Ariana shrunk it all to the appropriate size. She said as long as the fairies were our guests, their shopping would be part of my work.

Once the fairies' immediate needs were met, we gathered around the break room table, even The Cat sat in on the conversation.

Since Ariana, Orsinius and I didn't know much about real fairies, Merlin explained that there were four groups in the fairy world: fairies, elves, goblins and gnomes. While the others tended to live peacefully, elves were obsessed with power. Lord Rust and his elves had attempted to overthrow the goblin rulers some years ago, and had been forced back, with many losses to his army.

My mother suggested an unjust war, an attack on a neighbour who didn't do anything to provoke it was a matter for her.

Merlin agreed, but said there was no point in taking away the elves unless the fairy government could be restored. That would require locating, and possibly rescuing Queen Rose, if she was alive. To find her he would need something of hers.

Primrose insisted she hadn't brought anything of the Queen's with her.

Merlin pointed out the baby was the Queen's child, and that she would not be harmed by being the centre of a location spell.

With strange words, and magical powders, and a saucer full of water, Merlin was able to conjure an image of the Queen. She was obviously badly injured, and in some kind of dungeon.

"From seeing the image, can you bring her here?" Merlin asked.

Ariana held her hands out in front of her, and closed her eyes. Instantly, Queen Rose appeared, lying in Ariana's open hands.

"I can heal her," Ariana said.

"No," Merlin answered. "You've already used far too much magic today. Let's not risk catastrophic side-effects. We will do this the slow way. I will make a healing elixir. Miss Primrose, you have double duty, I am afraid. You will care for both your princess and your queen. I will give you medicine to give her and soon she will be well, and we will be able to take the next steps to restoring her to her throne."

My mother said we should keep a guard over all three fairies, in case Lord Rust's men came searching for them. The other adults agreed.

The Cat leapt up on the shelf beside the doll's house.

"Are you willing to guard them?" Ariana asked.

The Cat purred.

"That big beast?" Primrose said. "What if it tries to eat us?"

"It won't," Ariana said. "The Cat is a powerful magical creature, which once helped us save the world. If it chooses to guard you, you will be safe."

"Perhaps, I should bring Excalibur, and guard as well," Orsinius said quietly.

Primrose's eyes widened. She looked around the group. There we were: Lady Justice, the next Lady Justice, the world's most famous and powerful magician, the world's most powerful witch, The Cat, and a wisp who was guardian to some of the most famous mythical objects in history.

"I'm just a nursery maid. I don't belong among heroes, and mages, and judges, even the servant who sweeps the floor here is powerful."

Ariana smiled. "I'm just a hairdresser," she said. "An ordinary person like you. You're welcome here at my workplace, and among us. We are friends to each other, and now we are friends to you."

So that's how I became a not-quite-apprentice hairdresser, and the person who did supply runs for the Queen Rose, Princess Aster, and of course, Primrose, the nursery-maid who did not understand how courageous and important she was.

Spy

Primrose carefully followed Merlin's instructions, giving the queen half a drop of healing potion each morning and night. Her new friends made sure she, the queen and Princess Aster had everything they needed. Queen Rose gradually regained her strength.

When all of the fairies' new friends were gathered, the discussion quickly became about how to find out what was happening in the Fairy Kingdom.

"We need a spy," Queen Rose said. "Someone not well known, who will not draw attention."

Everyone looked at Primrose.

Primrose blushed. "I'm just a nursery maid," she said. "I wouldn't know how to be a spy. I look after the baby, that's all."

"All you would have to do would be to go there," Merlin said, gently. "We can watch you from a distance."

"I will go with you," Orsinius said. "I may not be able to go right into the kingdom, but I can wait nearby, with Excalibur, so you can call if you need help."

The Cat leapt up on the table beside Primrose. The Cat would go too.

"I can place a protection barrier over you so no-one can harm you, and give you extra strength and stamina as well. I haven't used magic today, so that small amount won't have side effects," Ariana said. "I can even make Orsinius temporarily invisible to fairies and elves, apart from you and the Queen."

"And Queen Rose and I can watch from here. All I need s some item that belongs to you, such as the necklace you wear. I won't hurt it," Merlin added.

Primrose did not believe she was capable, but if all her new friends would help, she would do it.

Ariana placed a hand over Primrose and closed her eyes a moment.

"Now you are stronger, than usual, and cannot be harmed for the next two days. I hope you won't be gone that long, but it's best to be sure." She did the same with both Orsinius and The Cat.

Then The Cat, Orsinius, and Primrose all entered the Interim, to move almost instantly to the Fairy Kingdom.

With Orsinius close by, and The Cat walking by her side, Primrose walked through the streets of the town she knew. The castle looked the same as it always did, except, instead of fairy guards, there were elf guards at the gate. Primrose didn't try to get too close. She didn't want to draw attention to herself.

She went to her parents' home. As soon as she knocked on the door, her mother grabbed her arm and dragged her inside. Her parents told her the elves were looking for everyone who worked in the castle. They were searching for the baby, and for the queen, who had somehow escaped from their dungeon.

Primrose asked if they knew what had happened to the fairy army or the castle guard. Her parents told her no-one knew where they were. They told her to run away quickly before she was caught.

A moment later there was another knock on the door. A loud voice demanded entrance. Primrose's mother went to the door.

An elf soldier asked, "Do you have a visitor in your house?"

"No. Just my husband and I are here."

"A person was seen entering your home."

"That was me, I just went out gathering food, some dew and some pollen, to bake bread."

"Your house will have to be searched."

The Cat, which had been sitting beside the house, swiped the elf soldier with a paw, sending him flying. The Cat's eyes glowed yellow, and the elf flew further than could be expected to be possible.

"Go now," Primrose's mother said, "before he regains consciousness."

"Come with me. I have friends who can help us," Primrose begged.

"No. We have friends here. Just tell me, is the princess safe? You were looking after her?"

"Yes, and the queen too. She sent me to find out how things are here."

"Things are bad. The soldiers have all run away. There is no-one left to fight back. Perhaps they will come back and fight if they know the Queen is safe."

Primrose ran back to Orsinius,

Two elves were yelling at The Cat. Orsinius' invisible hand picked up one and put him on roof of a nearby fairy house. The Cat swiped the other with a paw.

"Time to go, I think," Primrose said,

The three of them re-entered the Interim, and returned to Ariana's hairdressing salon.

"They all ran away," Queen Rose said. "Primrose, the nursery maid has been braver than my whole army. What are we going to do?"

"We're going to make a plan," Merlin said.

The Queen's Return

The scent of magic preceded them.

Queen Rose of the fairies rode on a sleek black cat. Above her flew Primrose, the nursery maid. At one side walked the great wizard Merlin, and Orsinius Wishlet, a wisp, guardian of mythical treasures, carrying Excalibur. On the other side, walked Lady Justice, her pearlescent wings folded, carrying her razor sharp scimitar, alongside the powerful witch Ariana Sutton.

Using the Interim, or Ariana's thought magic, they could have simply appeared in the fairy village. Instead, they chose to walk through the nearby forest.

As they walked, fairy soldiers and castle guards who had been hiding in the forest, fell into line and walked behind them.

They entered the village, the larger beings carefully avoiding stepping on houses.

Fairies came out of their houses and greeted their returning queen with cheers.

With the volume of her voice magically enhanced, Queen Rose called out from in front of the castle: "Lord Rust, you and your elves will leave the castle and leave the fairy lands immediately, on fear of penalty of imprisonment or death."

An elf messenger came out of the castle. "Lord Rust claims this castle and the whole land as his right, as his ancestors were cheated in the Great Settlement of the fae wars in time immemorial."

Lady Justice held out her hand, and a massive, ancient, book appeared, open, in her hand. She said: "Time immemorial is more remembered than Lord Rust believes. According to the record of my ancestor who mediated the Great Settlement, the elves gained a greater area of land than any of the other fae folk, on the promise that they would never again invade another of the fae nations. By right all elves must not enter fairy lands unless invited, and military actions are banned. Lord Rust and all elves will disarm and follow the Queen's orders immediately, or magical justice will be enforced."

The sun glinted on her sword.

The elf messenger dropped his sword, and started running. Other elves, seeing this, did the same.

Lord Rust had still not exited the castle.

The Queen called out again, but he still did not appear.

Ariana pointed to the ground in front of the castle gate, and Lord Rust appeared there, looked around, and tried to run but found himself unable to move.

Lady Justice lifted her sword, but the Queen called out, "No. Please imprison him, as I was imprisoned by him."

Lady Justice consulted briefly with Ariana, and Lord Rust found himself inside a very pink doll's house. He tried to leave, but found there was some kind of magical barrier preventing him. A teenaged girl who looked human, was watching the doll's house, while gently rocking a baby fairy in a nutshell.

"Lord Rust, I presume," Andy Justice said. "If you're here, I guess I can take Princess Aster home now." The girl, with the baby, disappeared into the Interim. Seconds later, she appeared beside the fairy castle. She gave the baby to Primrose, who carefully took her inside.

Minutes later, the Queen's standard was once more flying high over the castle.

Queen Rose appeared on the balcony, as fairies cheered, cried, and hugged each other.

"Today is a day of celebration," the Queen told her people. "Today things are back as they should be. We have to thank our magical guests who came to help us overthrow the invaders. Lady Justice, Andromeda Justice, Ariana Sutton, the Wizard Merlin, Orsinius Wishlet, and The Cat are forever welcome in our lands."

Fairies continued to cheered again.

The Queen continued, "Even greater thanks go to one of our own. Primrose, nursery maid to Princess Aster, not only saved the princess, but also negotiated with our new friends, arranged my rescue and courageously came here as a spy so we would know how to plan our return. Primrose is fond of saying she is just a nursery maid. Today, I declare her, our official Hero, the princess' protector, and my trusted advisor."

There were more riotous cheers, and in the crowd, Primrose's mother wept tears of pride and joy.

"I declare today a feast day, which will be remembered annually in honour of the great Hero Primrose," the Queen declared.

At that moment, Merlin threw some coloured dust in the air, muttered some strange words, and the sky filled with fireworks.

Ariana closed her eyes a moment, and tables filled with wonderful foods appeared all around the village.

Some fairies brought out musical instruments, and a celebration began which lasted late into the night.

Cat

The black cat sat between the curtain and the glass of the window, and gazed out at the mundane world of humans.

He thought back over how he'd come to be here, as much as he remembered.

There had been the witch. Not the one he was with now. The one long ago. He had known her when he walked on two legs. He had a name then. What was it?

He had argued with the witch. What about? His memory of that time was so vague, like thinking in a fog.

The witch had died. She'd been hanged. He remembered watching her body swaying. By that time, he was already a cat.

Had he denounced her? Had she cursed him, turned him into a cat?

Years swirled on, countries, faces. He'd been hungry. He'd been full. Sometimes, he'd lived on the street, and sometimes he'd lived in the country. He'd caught vermin on ships travelling from continent to continent. Sometimes he'd chosen humans or human-like creatures to live with. He'd always been the one to make the choice.

There had been witches, wizards, vampires, and creatures he could not identify. Occasionally, there'd been a human.

Some of them were imprinted in his memory. He remembered with fondness a simple peasant woman who had very little, but had happily shared her scarcity with him. He had hunted rabbits and brought them home for them both to eat. Occasionally, he'd used his powers to confuse the landlord and get her out of paying the rent when she had no money.

Other just faded like smoke. Many of them were magical practitioners, or lived on the fringe of magic. His previous "owner" was a thief and a purveyor of magical objects, and all things weird.

It was far from the strangest being he had lived with.

How many years had he been alive? One hundred? Two hundred? Three hundred? More? He did not know.

How long had it taken him to realise he was immortal? He could not remember. Had he been immortal when he walked on two legs? Or was it something that had come when he became a cat?

He'd seen plagues, wars and disasters. He'd seen countries rise in power then fall to insignificance. He'd seen so many humans who harmed others, and so many who were kind.

His current "owner" was a strange one.

She was the most powerful witch the world had ever known. He could feel the power radiating from her.

With all of that power, instead of ruling the world, she was cutting hair for a living. She lived in a tiny flat behind her hairdressing salon. She was kind and respectful to people around her. Power had not made her arrogant or selfish. When he'd met her, he'd lent her his power to overthrow a witch who meant harm to others. He'd known that kind of witch before. His witch, that one he'd known when he walked on two legs had been one of those. Had he been as bad? Perhaps she hadn't been bad at all. Perhaps, the argument he'd had with had been because he was bad. He did not know.

This witch he was with now was as different from them as light was from dark, as cold was from heat.

She had powerful friends who seemed to think the same way she did. The being who swept up the hair in her hairdressing studio was guardian to both Excalibur and the

Holy Grail. The apprentice she was teaching to cut hair was the future Lady Justice. The great wizard Merlin and Lady Justice herself were among her friends.

Apart from a doll's house in the store room which acted as jail for a criminal elf lord, the hair salon looked like any of the human businesses in the street. The customers all looked like regular humans, although The Cat could see through any glamour and knew that many were covering wings, or horns or other things that made them appear different.

The Cat felt safe with this powerful witch and her powerful friends, in their strange almost-human world. He felt safer than he could remember, but of course, so much of his memory was lost in the haze.

Of all the people he had encountered in all his years and all his journeys, he was sure that this witch, perhaps with help from her friends, would be the one who could finally help him.

If only he could find a way to communicate with her, to ask her.

He needed to know who he was, what his name was, what kind of a man he had been. He needed to know if he could go back to being whatever he was before he was a cat.

All he had to do was find a way to ask her, and be courageous enough to handle the answer.

Dream

Ariana was captured by villagers, dragged out to the hanging tree, and felt the rope over her neck.

No. She stopped it there.

She'd been having this dream or one like it over and over since she'd found out about her family's connection with witchcraft.

No, that wasn't quite right. She'd been having dreams about witches since then. She'd been having this specific dream since she, Merlin and The Cat, with support from their friends, had defeated her ancestor Lady Arabella March.

A lot of things had changed since then. She had gained Lady Arabella's power, on top of the considerable power she already had. The Cat had chosen to live with her. The magical community had come to see her as a leader, alongside Merlin, Lady Justice, and Orsinius Wishlet. She'd had the power to do anything she wanted, and being the only living heir to Lady Arabella, the money to anything. She'd chosen to go back to her hair salon.

Orsinius had decided to continue working for her. He had gone from being known as a nuisance, a thief, as all wisps were known to be, to being the guardian of some of the world's most powerful objects.

And the dreams had started. She'd been so disturbed by them she'd consulted Merlin and learned the art of lucid dreaming: to step in and change her own dreams.

Now, she removed her own noose. She turned to the gathered crowd, and told them to stop this insanity. She demanded to know what evidence they had against her.

At the back of the crowd, she saw a shadowy figure. A man, in black hat, trousers, shirt, and cloak. A man who seemed to hang back so as not to be noticed.

As she looked at him, the crowd froze, and the man called out to her. "Who am I? Tell me my name. Tell me my story. Give me my identity back."

His cloak swirled as he turned and left. The crowd began moving and chattering, apparently unaware that each person had been completely still and silent for at least a minute.

Ariana took control of the dream again, and the people moved aside to create a path for her to run through, following where the man in the cloak had disappeared.

She ran and ran, out past the edge of the village. She found a tiny cottage, with herbs growing in front. Something told her this was the place. Ariana opened the door, but the man wasn't there. Instead, she found a black cat, which looked identical to The Cat. Its glowing green eyes bored into her.

Ariana jerked awake. The Cat was, lying on top of her, also jerked awake.

"Sorry to disturb you," she said to The Cat. "I had a weird dream. I think you were in it, or some ancestor of yours.

The Cat looked at her, eyes glowing.

"You always look as if you know something. As if you've got a story to tell. I wish I knew what it was," Ariana said.

The Cat continued to stare.

"I don't know about you, but I'm going to try to get back to sleep," Ariana said, and laid back on her side.

The Cat again made itself comfortable, and began to purr.

Ariana drifted off to sleep again. She was back in that house. There was a big pot of something bubbling on a fire. Was that a cauldron? An authentic witch's cauldron? She supposed a cauldron was just a cooking pot then. There was no way to be sure it was a witch's house.

The black cat, which looked so much like The Cat ran past and out the door. She followed.

Exiting the house, she found herself somewhere completely different. She was on a sailing ship. The sea was churning. The man in the black cloak was standing on the deck, at the bow end of the ship. She was closer to the stern. The sailors on board froze, as the villagers had done, and the man called out to her, "Who am I? Tell me my name." His cape swirled and he vanished. The sailors moved again, and the black cat ran past, carrying a mouse in its mouth.

"Rumplestiltskin," Ariana said. No. That wasn't right. That was the fairytale character, who spun straw to gold and demanded the queen's first-born child.

Who was this man? What did he have to do with a black cat, that looked so much like The Cat?

"I don't know who you are. Why do you think I would know?" She called out to where the man had been.

Ariana rolled on to her other side, dislodging The Cat, who had to retake his place on top of her.

"No more. I'm leaving here." Ariana said in her dream.

Taking control of the dream, she moved to her own time, to her own hairdressing salon, and started cutting hair for a regular customer.

The Cat leapt up on its favourite shelf and watched her. "Tell me who I am," The Cat said.

Ariana suddenly woke and sat upright.

The Cat fell into her lap, on its back and scrambled to roll over back on its feet.

"What are you?" Ariana asked.

The Cat stared back at her, eyes glowing.

She realised that was what he wanted to know.

Mirror

Merlin, Ariana, Orsinius and The Cat sat around the table in Ariana's kitchen. Or rather, the people sat around the table, and The Cat sat on it.

Ariana explained to the others about her dream, and The Cat's desire to remember who he truly was.

Merlin was quiet for a moment, then said, "I had actually come to seek Mr Wishlet's assistance in a quest. That is, in his capacity as Guardian of Mythical Objects. However, I believe the results of this quest may provide the answers Mr Cat is looking for. Mr Wishlet, will you assist me?"

Ariana and The Cat both looked expectantly at Orsinius.

He looked around the room, then back at Merlin and answered, "I will help, of course. What do I need to take with me and when will we leave?"

"You need only take yourself, and we leave immediately, if you are willing. Miss Sutton, Mr Cat, please excuse our absence. We will return momentarily."

Merlin muttered a few words in an obscure language, and he and Orsinius disappeared.

The Cat looked questioningly at Ariana.

"Don't ask me," she said. "But their other quests have retrieved Excalibur, and the Holy Grail, so I wouldn't be surprised by anything now."

Orsinius and Merlin arrived at what Orsinius recognised from a previous quest as an archaeological dig site.

"Same as before, Mr Wishlet," Merlin said. I will enter, and will point to the object we need to retrieve. You will use the Interim to take the object. On this occasion, however, I will give you a cloth to cover the object. Do not look directly at it. Cover it, and take it. Keep it covered."

Orsinius nodded his assent.

He held back while he saw Merlin greet a person who seemed to be in charge of the dig.

"Dr Merle, I'm so pleased you could come," the archaeologist said.

"The pleasure is all mine. I heard you had unearthed some amazing finds," Merlin replied.

They walked together, to a set of tables, under a temporary shelter, where the archaeologist began showing items recovered from the dig.

Orsinius waited a couple of minutes, then checked no-one was watching, and slipped into the Interim. He followed where Merlin and the archaeologist had gone. They were looking closely at an old vase. Merlin had his hands behind his back, and was pointing at an object on the table behind him.

As in a previous quest, the humans had failed to know which of the things they had recovered was truly important.

Orsinius noted where Merlin was pointing, and tried not to look at the object as he covered it, but he found a quick glance was necessary to see where he was throwing the cover. In that glance, he saw a reflection of himself in his old life, as a thief, stealing things from humans. Worst of all, he saw himself stealing from Ariana.

He threw the cloth over the awful object, then darted outside to hide near where Merlin had left him. He sat behind a large rock, where no-one from the dig would notice him, and cried.

He didn't hear Merlin approach.

"You looked, Mr Wishlet?" Merlin asked gently.

"I tried not to, but I could nott see where to put the cover. I saw..."

"I know what you saw, my friend. But remember, if it were not for the past, you would not have the present. Are you happy in the present?"

"I am very happy."

"Then dry your tears. Yesterday is gone and cannot be changed. Today is good, and tomorrow may be, too."

Orsinius nodded, and stood up. Merlin handed him a large handkerchief, and Orsinius wiped his eyes and blew his nose."

Merlin muttered more strange words, and they were back in Ariana's kitchen.

Orsinius carefully put the object on the table.

Merlin said, "This is the Mirror of Mim. It belonged to Mimir, whose name led to English word 'memory'. Like all magical mirrors, it tells the truth. It does not attempt to be kind. Mr Cat, if you truly wish to know the truth of your past, you may look in this mirror. Be aware, however, that you may have chosen to forget some things, or to imagine those things differently. From what you have been able to impart to Miss Sutton, we know you have lived a very long time. In a long life, there are very many opportunities for events that you may not wish to remember. Do you wish to look at the mirror?"

The Cat put his paw on the cloth covering the artefact.

"Then," Merlin said, "we shall all leave the room before you remove the cover. After you have looked, I request that you pull the cover back over it before you come out to us."

Merlin, Orsinius and Ariana left the room.

The Cat pulled the cover from the mirror.

As he looked, he saw himself, as a cat, then slowly, the image merged into a young man in a wizard's robe and hat.

He remembered himself as a young nobleman, who had displayed an affinity for magic. Disregarding his father's wishes, he'd apprenticed to a senior wizard.

When his father disinherited him, he planned to kill his father with magic. His father, however, also had some natural magic, and the young wizard wasn't strong enough alone.

He'd gone to a witch for help. It was the witch he'd earlier remembered hanging, the witch he'd thought must have been evil because he had a vague memory of her arguing with him. She'd refused to be part of murder. That was what they'd argued about.

He'd attacked her. His spell was to turn her into a cat, but she'd resisted, somehow she'd turned his curse back on him.

The witch had confessed the whole thing to the wizard's father, who had ordered her hanged.

Now the cat knew enough. He knew the spell and how to reverse it. He knew his name, and his heritage. He extended a paw and pulled the cover back over the mirror. This was enough memory to open channels in his mind, to allow him to access more of his power.

He thought of what he had done, how he'd tried to kill his own father, and as a result had caused the death of a witch who had done no harm, but only defended herself from him.

He'd suspected he'd known great evil, but not that he had been responsible for it.

Feeling a guilt he now believed would never be atoned, he leapt gently down from the table, and walked to the next room where the others were waiting.

With his newly-remembered power, he was able to speak telepathically to them.

"My name is Benwyn, and I choose to remain a cat. This is my penance, for a crime I do not wish to discuss."

Snake

Orsinius appeared in the hairdressing salon. He had been rushing through the Interim, and was gasping for breath.

"What's wrong?" Ariana asked.

"The snake. The one Lady Arabella had on her stick. The one I broke with Excalibur. I left the pieces in a pile near the entrance to my burrow. I did not know it could happen."

"You didn't know what could happen?"

"The snake. It joined itself together then it disappeared."

"I think we need the team back together," Ariana said.

Benwyn, the black cat, who had been sitting on the counter beside her, thought to them, "I will get Merlin and Lady Justice." He disappeared into the Interim.

"We need some things from your burrow," Ariana said, "but let's not have you run again."

She used her magic to transport them to Orsinius' burrow.

"All of the artefacts, I think. Because we don't know what we're really going to find."

"Even the..?"

"Even the Mirror of Mim, but please keep it covered."

Orsinius looked ashamed for a moment. "Will you carry it, please?" He asked.

"Did you look at it?"

Orsinius hung his head.

Ariana said, "Fair enough. We won't talk about it."

He said quietly, "It was when I was still a thief. I stole from you."

"When you stole something tiny from me, discovered me stuck in the Interim, and then saved my life? I'm so grateful for that. If you hadn't been there to steal, you wouldn't have found me. You might be ashamed of that, but I'm grateful. I'm glad of it."

Orsinius looked up at her. "I know now that stealing is bad."

"You're not the person you were then."

"When I was learning not to be a thief, Merlin told me what I was, was not who I would become."

"Well, he was right. You saved me. You've saved the world once or twice. You've saved all of reality. You're a hero. And you're the keeper of powerful magical objects. And you're my best friend. The past doesn't matter now. But yes, I'll carry the mirror, if you don't want to. Not because you have anything to be ashamed of, but because you're my friend."

Orsinius went to the back of the burrow, and returned with Excalibur, the Grail, and a velvet bag which held the Mirror of Mim.

Ariana brought them back to the hairdressing salon, as Merlin, Lady Justice and Benwyn arrived.

Orsinius told them about the snake disappearing.

Ariana added, that as Lady Arabella had kept much of her power, and possibly some of her personality, in the snake, it could be a very dangerous thing to leave free.

Merlin said, "Mr Wishlet used Excalibur to break the snake before. That is a contact which could be used. Excalibur may help us scry for the snake."

On the table in Ariana's kitchen, they placed Excalibur. Ariana opened up the maps app on her phone and put it on the table beside the sword.

"Mixing old magic with new magic. This may prove better than paper maps," Merlin said, approvingly.

Ariana placed one hand on Excalibur, and one on the phone. The map moved, eventually stopping, with a glowing green dot over a point in Indonesia.

"I guess that's where we're going," Ariana said.

"Coffee first," Merlin said. "Not to have a rest, but as a boost to magic. You all know how drained we were after we dealt with Lady Arabella before. The snake has only a small amount of her power, but it will still be a formidable foe."

After coffee, Ariana used her thought magic to move them all to the point on the map.

They looked around, and then looked up.

They were beside a tower, with a pagoda roof, and a tall spire. Wrapped around the spire was a large silver-white snake, with glowing emerald eyes, and a green glow around it.

"That's a little bigger than the last time I saw it," Ariana said. "Does anyone have a plan of attack?"

Orsinius drew Excalibur, and Lady Justice drew her scimitar.

Benwyn leapt up and pulled the bag with the mirror out of her hand. He pulled the mirror free, and climbed up the tower, with it in his mouth.

"Did anyone know he could do that?" Lady Justice asked. The others shrugged or shook their heads.

On the roof of the tower, Benwyn simply sat, and held the mirror where the snake could see it.

No one watching could see what the snake saw in the mirror, but it slipped from the tower.

That allowed the others to reach it.

Merlin raised his staff, Ariana stared at the snake aiming a magical attack at it, while Orsinius and Lady Justice both slashed with their swords. By the time Benwyn was down from the tower, the snake was once more a small silver snake

90

ornament, broken in pieces. Merlin distributed the pieces one to Lady Justice, one to Orsinius and one to himself.

Merlin asked, "Mr Wishlet, would please go to the edge of the border, and drop your piece of the snake into unreality?"

Orsinius readily agreed.

Merlin continued, "I will drop my piece into an active volcano. Lady Justice, I know you will keep a record of this action. I leave it to you to choose if you will place your piece with your records."

Lady Justice answered, "Thank you Merlin. Sketches and a written record will suffice. I will drop this at the deepest part of the ocean, so the pieces cannot reunite."

Merlin turned to Ariana, "Miss Sutton, I have chosen to not break the snake into smaller pieces for you and Mr Benwyn to dispose of. In his current form Mr Benwyn is limited, and because of your familial relationship with Lady Arabella, there is a danger of prolonged contact with the snake doing you harm."

Ariana nodded. "I'm more than happy trust your judgement. I know enough about magic to know that I don't know much about it at all."

"That is indeed, so I won't trouble you to take Mr Wishlet, Lady Justice or myself away from here. I could ask you to simply take yourself and Mr Benwyn back to your salon, and then do no further magic for the day, or perhaps even the week. Oh, and drink more coffee. It might only be mildly magical, but it does help replenish what you have expended."

Ariana took the mirror from Benwyn and carefully placed it back in its bag. "Would you like me to take this back to the salon for now? I can take it back to your place when I've recovered."

Orsinius held out his hand. "No," he said. "I am not afraid of the past. I can take it now."

He took the bag, and disappeared into the Interim. Merlin and Lady Justice also disappeared.

"I guess it's home time for us, too, Benwyn," Ariana said.

She took them back to the salon, and they drank coffee together..

Claire

Claire began to cross the road.

A car swerved to avoid hitting her. The driver sounded the horn. From the front passenger window she could see a middle finger extended, the modern world's universal symbol for "up yours."

Clairs smiled. Although the car was already far ahead of her, she heard the scream as the hand, now with a broken finger, was pulled back into the car.

The world had changed, but so had Claire of Canterbury. She would not accept disrespect.

Once, she had passively allowed herself to be executed, at the command of Lord Harald, with the full support of the villagers. Those villagers had come to her for years for her to heal their ailments, help ease troubled sleep, assist in their births. Then, when she was accused of witchcraft, those who had benefitted from her craft turned against her.

Their betrayal had not been the worst. No, there was one other she held responsible for all of it.

She looked at the palm of her hand. The arrow she had drawn there moved slightly, and she turned to follow the direction it pointed. Currently, she was limited to the spells she could perform without her potions, without magical objects, and without her grimoire. She knew, however, her objective would have all of those things, and she would be able to claim them, once she took her revenge.

She entered the hairdressing salon, quickly noted that neither the staff nor patrons were actually human, and demanded, "Deliver to me Benwyn, son of Lord Harald of Canterbury."

From another room, a sleek black cat with piercing green eyes leapt up on to a bench beside her, and held her with its gaze.

He was still a cat. How many years ago had his spell failed and turned him, instead of her, into a cat? Had he not yet found a way to undo it?

The Cat, Benwyn, stared at her, as if staring right into her soul.

His being a helpless cat made it all too easy. She saw a pair of sharp scissors, picked them up, and was about to plunge them into the cat, when she suddenly found herself unable to move. She was standing there, arm raised, unable to do anything.

Now, at last, she paid some more attention to the beings in the room.

There was a small creature, with a long beard and a bald head. He looked like a wisp, but carried himself with more dignity and strength than any wisp she had ever met.

There was a woman with large pearlescent, white wings, who was now standing, holding a scimitar she recognised as belonging to Lady Justice. This was not the Lady Justice of her time, but surely a descendant. A younger woman, with multi-coloured wings stood beside Lady Justice, Claire now realised the resemblance between the two and that she was attempting murder in front of both the current and the future Lady Justice.

None of these beings were holding her, however. That was the witch. She looked like any ordinary human, but now Claire realised this was no ordinary witch.

"I can't let you harm my friend," the woman said quietly. "Clearly, you are upset about something, but this is not the way to deal with it."

The woman walked over to Claire and gently removed the scissors from her hand. She pointed to a chair.

Claire found herself able to move again, and obediently sat in the chair.

The witch Ariana, introduced herself, and the wisp Orsinius Wishlet, Lady Justice and Andromeda Justice.

"I gather you already know Benwyn, so perhaps you could tell us who you are, and why you want to harm our friend."

"I am Claire, witch of Canterbury. I was killed, hanged, by Lord Harald, Benwyn's father, because of something Benwyn did."

"You don't seem to be particularly dead now," Ariana said, "so there must be more to your story."

"An extremely powerful witch named Lady Arabella March brought me back to life. She said she wanted powerful witches by her side and would call me when she wanted me. She did not call, and I sought her out, but was unable to find her. So I decided to seek out my own revenge while I awaited her. I must warn you, she is a very powerful witch, and will not take kindly to you detaining me."

The witch Ariana smiled, a condescending smile Claire planned to wipe away whenever her new patron, Lady Arabella, would reappear.

"Lady Arabella won't take kindly or even unkindly to anything," Ariana said. "You see, she tried to destroy reality, and steal my power, so we had to stop her. There's no way to bring her back. I can see you have trouble believing me. Instead of trying to find her, try to locate her power. Go ahead."

Claire concentrated, and looked at the arrow drawn on her hand. The arrow pointed directly at Ariana.

"You are her heir?" Claire asked, faintly.

"Heir and executioner, with help from my friends, including Benwyn. I don't know what happened between you and Benwyn. I don't know who or what he was before he became

95

a cat, or before he helped us defeat Lady Arabella, but I know who he is now. He has helped save the world, save reality itself, more than once. He does not have to stay in the form of a cat, but chooses to do so as a penance for a crime he chose not to disclose to any of us. Whatever he might have been, whatever he might have done, now he is good, and now he is our friend."

"You killed Lady Arabella and stole her power, I believe that much. I refuse to believe she as anything but good."

"See for yourself," Ariana sad, and placed her hand on Claire's forehead. She showed Claire all that had lead up to the death of Lady Arabella.

Claire hung her head for a moment, then said, "She was good to me. She brought me back to life."

"Did you loan her any of your own power?" Lady Justice asked.

"I did, but it was returned back to me."

"She didn't return it to you. It returned when she died," Lady Justice said. "She brought you, and possibly other witches, back so she could feed off your power, like a vampire. Her whole existence was about gaining power, so much so that she was willing to sacrifice the entirety of this reality, and possibly others, to gain more. That is why we had to stop her. That is why her own power was passed to her heir, who was already a powerful witch in her own right. That is why the power she took from you was returned to you. If she were still alive, she would have kept your power, continued to drain you until you died again. Now Benwyn has been a cat for hundreds of years as penance. Whatever his crimes, I declare, as only I can, that his penalty has been paid."

Benwyn leapt from the counter, and mid-air gained the shape of the young wizard he had once been. His friends noticed that in taking the form, he had dressed himself in robes similar to those habitually worn by Merlin.

"I am sorry," he said. "My actions were selfish and unthinking, but it was never my intention they would lead to your death. I loved you. Through all these years, I have continued to love you."

"And I loved you, but what you planned was wrong. That was why I went to your father and told him everything."

"And my father, being my father, decided the solutions was to execute you."

"Yes."

"My father is not here. This is a new and changed world. We can have a life now that we could never have had then."

"How do we make a life in this place? Everything we had is gone. My books are gone."

"We make a life in any way we like. Between us, even without your books, we have enough magic to make any good thing possible."

Benwyn opened the door out to the street, and he and Claire walked through it.

Lady Justice was about to follow when Ariana stopped her. "No," she said. "Her anger wasn't hatred, but betrayed love. Benwyn's safe, and they will be fine."

Lady Justice was not easily convinced. "For the past five hundred years, he's been a cat and she's been dead. How will they be fine?"

"They'll find their way, and they know how to find us if they ever need our help."

Birthday Party

Princess Aster was sleepy, she was lying on the large swing in the palace grounds, with her head on her nursery maid's lap.

"Tell me the story again," she said sleepily, "about how you saved me and flew all the way to the human city and put me to sleep in a nut shell, and how you made all the new friends who helped us come home safely."

"I think you've just about told the whole story yourself," Primrose, the nursery maid, and the Queen's Hero, answered.

"You must have been very brave."

"Mostly I was very frightened. When Lord Rust and his elves took over and took Queen Rose prisoner, I was more frightened than I've ever been. But I had the most important job in the kingdom, and I had to think about that, not about how scared I was."

"What was the most important job in the kingdom?"

"I was a nursery maid to the Princess, and I had to make sure she was safe. So i took you and flew away, not knowing where I was going, and afraid I wouldn't find safety."

"And then you found the new friends."

"And then I found our new friends, and they gave us a little house to be safe in, and I looked after you there."

"But that's not all you did."

"What do you mean?"

"Bartleby said you came back as a spy to help my mother escape, and you looked after her there too, because she was hurt. Then helped our new friends and my mother to take the kingdom back, and lock up Lord Rust, too."

"Bartleby is very talkative, for a butler. I might have done some of those things. I couldn't have done any of it without the help of our friends."

"I was a baby then. I don't remember our friends, I only know what you told me about them. I want to meet them all, the witch, the wisp, the cat, the wizard and Lady Justice, and the Junior Justice, too."

"What if we ask the Queen to invite them to your birthday celebration. They are as much friends to her as they are to you and I. Actually, they're friends to the whole kingdom, because they helped free the kingdom from the elves."

"I would like that. Yes, please can we ask my mother?"

Neither the Princess, nor the nursery maid knew that behind a nearby tree, an elf spy was listening.

When a messenger went out from the palace to the human city with the invitation, spies followed, and found the location of the house, with the hairdressing salon in front, where Ariana the witch lived and worked.

One spy attempted to gain access to the store room where Lord Rust was held prisoner in a magically-transformed doll house. The wisp Orsinius Wishlet caught the spy, and threw him outside.

Ariana read the invitation, the told Orsinius about it, then used her thoughts to pass the invitation on to Lady Justice and her daughter Andy, to the wizard Merlin, and to the wizard Benwyn, who had been a cat at the time of Primrose's great flight to freedom.

On the day of Princess Aster's birthday, the friends gathered and went to the forest together. The wizards were in their best robes. The women were in bright colourful dresses. Orsinius Wishlet was neatly dressed, with his long beard carefully combed, and his head polished until it shone.

Aster was delighted to meet the friends she couldn't remember, but had heard about so often. "But where is the fierce cat who fought for our kingdom?" she asked.

Benwyn smiled, and was instantly transformed into a sleek black cat with piercing green eyes.

The Princess squealed with delight.

The whole kingdom joined in feasting and music and dancing long into the night.

While the friends were at the party, however, the elves saw their chance. They broke into the hairdressing salon, and went to the storeroom where the spy had seen Lord Rust imprisoned.

The doll house, and Lord Rust were no longer there.

After a futile search of the whole salon and house, the elves went home discouraged.

In another part of the city, a seller of strange, archaic and occult items entered his large vault at the end of the day. This was where he kept his most precious things.

In a corner of the vault sat the doll house. Inside, Lord Rust was begging, pleading, and offering bribes to be released.

Augustus Wishlet, wisp, thief, and shopkeeper, picked up an old human skull, his most prized possession.

"Sorry about the noise, Ned," he said. "I thought an imprisoned elf lord would be an impressive addition to my collection, so I took him as soon as Ariana and the others left. Actually, he is just annoying. I should never have stolen him. I will return him, I promise."

Key

The raven pushed against the door. A bell rang as it opened, and again as it closed behind him. The room he entered was empty, but he could hear voices from a back room.

A female voice was saying, "Between uni and work here, I thought I had enough to do, but Mum wants me to start studying the family historical records now. So that's why I've brought this volume. I need to study in my break."

Another, somewhat older, female voice said, "If you need to reduce your hours here, I'm happy to do that."

The first voice answered, "Oh no. My work here helps me to still feel normal, you know, not so much like I've got this massive weight of destiny on top of me. Especially since I finally gave in and decided to do uni part time, while still planning to do hairdressing apprenticeship."

She was greeted with murmurs of agreement.

With a hopping kind of gait, the raven made his way to where he heard the sound coming from.

Sitting around a table, drinking the mildly magical liquid coffee, were three beings.

There was a teenager, of a species that seemed familiar, but he could not quite place. Her multi-coloured wings were folded casually behind her back. There was a wisp, with a shining bald head, huge ears, and long grey beard, an inconsequential being. Why others deigned to drink any beverage with him was beyond the raven's understanding.

The third was the witch he had come to find. He could feel the power radiating from her. He was definitely in the right place.

The younger woman said, "Hey look, it's a crow, carrying a key."

The raven dropped the sparkling gold key he was carrying, and said, "Not a crow, an Australian Raven. We're related, but not the same. My name is Corvin Ravenwing. Am I in the presence of the witch Ariana Sutton?"

The adult woman answered, "Yes, I'm Ariana. How can I help you?"

Corvin said, "I am, or rather was, the solicitor who managed property matters for Lady Arabella March. I understand you are her heir?"

Ariana said, "I believe so."

"You inherited her power. Correct?"

"Yes, I did. What's this about?"

"And Lady Justice arranged transfer of her physical possessions from the human world?

"Yes."

"I am here to deliver the rest of your inheritance, the magical property of Lady Arabella, of course you also inherit her title and are now Lady Ariana."

He picked up the glittery key, flew the short distance to stand on the table, and dropped the key beside Ariana's coffee mug. He said, "This transaction requires witnesses, may I ask if your associates here will witness that I have given you this key?"

Both of the other beings there agreed that they witnessed it.

"I will need your names for the record," the raven said.

The girl said, "I'm Andromeda Justice. You can call me Andy, everyone does."

The raven seemed frozen for a moment, then practically squeaked, "You are the Junior Justice?" That's why she seemed to be of a species he should recognise. He had made a career of avoiding making applications to her mother.. "Please accept my apologies for not addressing you first. I meant no breach of protocol."

Andy shrugged, and said, "I didn't know it was a breach, if it was. I'm not here as Lady Justice's daughter. Here, I'm just an apprentice hairdresser, and a part-time uni student."

Corvin said, "Oh, I see." He did not see. He did not understand what the world's most powerful witch and the Junior Justice were doing in this nondescript place.

He turned his attention to the wisp. At least he couldn't make a faux pas there. A wisp would never be of import. He said, "And you, sir, are?"

"Orsinius Wishlet," the wisp replied politely.

Ariana had detected the disdain in the raven's voice, and followed her friend's statement up with, "Orsinius is appointed Guardian of Mythical Objects, if you need his title."

The raven now seemed shocked. "Guardian of…?"

Ariana smiled, "Oh yes. He was appointed by Lady Justice and Merlin as Guardian. Excalibur, the Holy Grail, and the Mirror of Mim, in his care at the moment. Merlin and Lady Justice wouldn't trust anyone else with the care of such powerful objects."

The raven began to feel his legs shake. Even the wisp wasn't just a wisp. Nothing in this place made sense.

"Are you OK there, Corvin?" Ariana asked. "Would you like a coffee?"

"Ah, no, thank you. I am unused to being among such powerful beings. If you have acknowledged receipt of the key, and you have no further questions, I will not impose on your time any longer."

"Oh, I do have questions," Ariana said, as she picked up the key. "What exactly is this the key to?"

"To all of Lady Arabella's magical property, of course," Corvin did not know why she would ask such a question. Why would such a powerful witch not know?

"So like a house, or something? Where is it?"

Corvin was thoroughly confused. How could she not know this? "It's a realm key. It opens the realm Lady Arabella created to store her property."

"And how do I use it?"

"It's a key. You put it in a keyhole and use it to unlock the door."

"Which door?"

Corvin ruffled his feathers, took a deep breath, and explained, as if to a child, "You put the key in any door, and turn it. The key will turn the door into a door to the realm it was created for. When you exit the realm, the door returns to its former usage."

"OK. Thanks. I think I've got that. So this is a realm only for the property Lady Arabella left, so anything on the other side of the door when I open it is now mine?"

"That is correct, yes."

"Thanks, Corvin. I appreciate your help."

"You are welcome, my lady. If you should ever require my legal services, feel free to call my name three times, to summon me."

Corvin bowed, and began his hopping walk to the edge of the table, when he heard a voice yelling from another room.

"Corvin! Corvin Ravenwing! Is that you?" The voice called out. "It's me Lord Rust. You did some work for me a while ago. Can you help me? These monsters have imprisoned me!"

Corvin tilted his head on its side. Dare he question these beings, now that he knew what they all were.

Ariana smiled. "To be clear," she said quietly, "Lady Justice imprisoned him. We are just his jailers."

Corvin shook his head. "Lady Justice does not take prisoners. I will not believe this unless I see her record of it."

"I can show you that," Andy said. She flicked through the pages of a huge book she had on the table in front of her. "Here we are. It wasn't long ago. The Fairy Queen was the victim, and she pleaded with my mother to have mercy, and not execute him."

Corvin hopped over to the book, and read. It was yet another impossible thing he'd discovered in this place of impossibilities.

"Imprisonment is a thing unknown in magical law," Corvin said. "Might I be permitted to speak to my client?"

"Go ahead," Ariana said. "I won't remove the magical barrier without Lady Justice's explicit order, but you are free to talk to him through the barrier."

Corvin hopped his way to the store room, where he found Lord Rust imprisoned in a pink plastic dolls' house.

He soon returned to the room where the three beings were seated, and asked, "When is my client allowed to be released from his prison?"

The three of them looked at each other as if each thought the other might know. Eventually, Ariana said, "I don't know. I will let him out when Lady Justice says to."

Andy looked at the record again and said, "She hasn't made any decision on that, but if you think it should be reviewed, you can always make an application to her."

Make an application to Lady Justice? On behalf of someone she'd already deemed guilty?

Corvin fainted.

A little later he woke, to find himself still on the table, with a tiny pillow placed under his head. All the other beings seemed to have gone.

The teenaged Junior Justice entered the room. "You're awake," she said. "Ariana said to check on you. She's got a client right now, and Orsinius is out doing odd jobs. Was it scary to think about seeing my mother? Is that why you fainted?"

"I... No. I mean... I..."

"It's OK. I think both Ariana and Orsinius used to be scared of her, until they got to know her. I never was, but she's my Mum, so I guess it would be weird if I was scared of her, wouldn't it? She's not really all that bad. I mean she won't show mercy if you don't deserve it. But you're just a lawyer doing a job for a client. So she'll listen to you. You might even convince her."

Corvin had not expected kindness from this creature. "Do you think I might?"

"You never know until you try."

After Ariana's client left, the raven made his way, hopping out the door.

Orsinius came back from his errands.

Ariana said to her friends, "Should we try out this key and see what's on the other side of the door?"

She chose the door between the hairdressing salon, and her private residence. She put the key in the lock, and turned it.

They entered and found themselves in a strange mansion, with large rooms and high ceilings, and with no windows.

There were endless shelves with ageing books of magic. There were potions and poisons, cauldrons and vials. There was one room filled with gold bars.

The three explored it all.

Eventually, they had seen everything.

Ariana sighed. "It would take a lifetime to read all those books," she said. "And I don't know that I want to mess around with potions and spells anyway. I like my thought magic. I suppose, one day, I might want to learn some of that other stuff. It's a resource if I ever need it. For now, though, I think I'm happy just to leave this all here."

"Perhaps, you should show this to Merlin, since he is still teaching you about magic," Orsinius said.

Ariana nodded, thoughtfully.

They returned through the door, and Ariana closed and locked it.

She thought for a moment to trust the key to Orsinius, but he had already been given so much unasked for responsibility.

Using her thought magic, she pressed the key into her arm, and it was absorbed. Should she ever need it, she would be able to open the door with the power of her thoughts.

"It's been a weird day. Coffee anyone?" Ariana asked.

Orsinius rushed to make it. He had become proud of his coffee making skill.

Parole

Corvin Ravenwing entered the room, in his usual hopping gait.

The pink dolls' house that was his client's cell was now on the table in the break room of the salon.

Sitting at the table were Lady Justice, and Andy, the Junior Justice. Behind them, making coffee, was Orsinius Wishlet the wisp, who was also Guardian of Mythical Objects.

On the table, as far as possible from the dolls' house, were three fairies, two adults and one infant. Lady Justice introduced them as the Fairy Queen Rose, the Fairy Hero and Nursemaid Primrose, and the infant Princess Aster.

He wondered, once more, why so many powerful beings would gather in this place. He also wondered what he, a simple solicitor, was doing in this intimidating company.

A door that apparently led to the residence attached to the business opened. Through the open doorway, Corvin could see that the door currently led to Lady Arabella's Realm, or perhaps he should now think of it as Lady Ariana's Realm. The witch herself, and a bearded wizard in long robes exited the room. Corvin was astonished to see the witch lock the door using only her hand, without the realm key he had recently provided her. The witch might have seemed unaware of many things, but she was far more powerful than even he had believed.

The wizard addressed Lady Justice, saying, "Miss Sutton and I have done as you requested." He turned to Corvin and said, "Mr Ravenwing, I don't believe we have met before. My name is Merlin. You may have heard of me."

Corvin had indeed heard of him.

Lady Justice said, "Mr Ravenwing, I have already found your client guilty, and imposed the sentence of imprisonment upon him. I understand you have an application to put before me, with regard to his punishment."

Corvin looked around the room at all the powerful beings who were assembled. He tried not to allow himself to quiver in fear, or his voice to quaver. He said, "My Lady, as imprisonment is previously unknown as a penalty for magical crime, I am uncertain of the protocol here. Please forgive me if I make a mistake here. I mean no disrespect. I have consulted my client, Lord Rust, and I understand he has been imprisoned for a year. While all his physical needs have been met, he has been isolated from his own people, and is in despair. I ask you to consider his release, or otherwise to make a ruling on how long he is to continue his punishment." He bowed so low he almost fell over into a somersault.

Lady Justice addressed the Fairy Queen, "Queen Rose, it was your request that I withheld the death penalty in this case, but rather imposed the penalty of loss of liberty. Do you have anything to say on this matter?"

The Queen bowed to Lady Justice, then said, "I am constantly grateful to you and your associates for my rescue, and for the protection of my child and the hero who saved her. I did ask that you imprison Lord Rust, in the same manner that he had imprisoned me. I was imprisoned for three months, and he has been for four times that amount of time. If there was a way to ensure he would not lead his elves in another attack on my people or my lands, I would be happy for him to be released." She bowed once more.

Lady Justice addressed Lord Rust. "Lord Rust, your crime ought to have brought the penalty of death, as crime in the magical world usually does. Instead, you have become the first magical being to ever be held in a prison of sorts. This is a thing frequently done in the human world. Another thing frequently done in human law is called parole. This is when a person who has been imprisoned is allowed to go free, but certain limitations are placed on them. I am inclined to set you free, but I will have limitations for you. I have asked Merlin and

Lady Ariana to create a device which will monitor your whereabouts, this was also inspired by something in the human justice system. If you agree to wear this device, I will be immediately notified if you should enter the fairy lands. I will also be notified if you give orders to other elves to enter the fairy lands. You will be unable to remove the device. If you agree to the condition of wearing this device, I will release you immediately."

Corvin saw a problem with that condition. Dare he speak up? Swallowing hard, he said, "Pardon my interruption, My Lady, but to arrive in his own lands from here, Lord Rust will have to travel through the fairy lands. Even using the Interim, he would still have to travel through for some very small amount of time."

The witch Ariana laughed. She actually laughed. Could she not understand the issue?

She said, "I can transport him home, immediately, without crossing the fairy lands."

Corvin stared in disbelief. Did she really have the power to do that?

Lady Justice nodded to Ariana, then said, "Your decision, Lord Rust?"

A tearful Lord Rust agreed to any and all conditions, anything to get out of the awful, pink plastic dolls' house.

Ariana said, "I've lifted the magical barrier imprisoning him."

She hadn't used any incantations, any mixed spells, or even any hand movements. She had simply said it was done. Corvin had never seen anything like this.

Merlin passed something shiny to the witch, who placed the item on top of the elf's head, where it seemed to disappear.

She said, "The device is installed."

Lady Justice asked if Lord Rust had anything more to say to the court before returning to his own lands.

He shook his head.

Lady Justice then told Ariana to send him home. Lord Rust simply disappeared.

Corvin jumped, then looked carefully where his client had stood.

Ariana smiled, "It's OK," she said. "He's home safe. I can send you after him, if you want to make sure."

Corvin backed slowly away from her. He said, "No. No. That won't be necessary."

He accidentally backed into the small fairy princess.

"Ouch, Mr Crow," Princess Aster squeaked.

He jumped again. Then turned to the princess and bowed. "I'm sorry Your Highness. But wait! I'm not a crow! Crows are tricksters, and thieves. I'm a raven!" He suddenly realised he was yelling at a literal child, not only that, but a Princess, and was certain he was about to lose his head.

The princess laughed. Everyone else in the room did as well.

"Sorry Mr Raven," Princess Aster said. "I didn't mean to hurt your feelings, but you knocked me over."

Corvin bowed, "I'm sorry, too, Your Highness, for knocking you over, and for losing my temper at you."

"It's OK Mr Raven."

To Primrose, Princess Aster said, "That's the house we lived in, isn't it? When I was a baby and you rescued me, and our friends helped us? Can I look at it now?"

Primrose smiled indulgently at the child. "It really belongs to Miss Andromeda, so if she says it's allowed, you're welcome to explore it."

Andy assented happily, and the child ran through the dolls' house, which had been first a sanctuary, and then a prison, and was now just a plastic toy once more.

Ariana looked around the gathered group. "I think it's about time for dinner. Are you all staying? Corvin, I have a fair idea what everyone else likes, but I don't know your dietary needs, will you tell me what you want?"

Corvin was surprised. He looked around the assembled group of powerful beings. He said, "Are you inviting me to join you for a meal?"

"Of course," Ariana said. "We're all friends here."

Joining in a luxurious meal that had simply appeared in front of him, Corvin realised he'd begun to understand why all these powerful beings would gather in such a place, after all.

Jack

Ariana was alone in the dark. It was black, strangely her environment was soft. She she was on a surface too unstable to stand on, so she was crawling, trying to find her way in a soft, velvet, black environment.

Something moved, a gigantic, green, eye, like a cat's eye, but far bigger than Ariana herself, opened, and stared at her.

She heard the voice of her friend Benwyn, who had lived many years as a cat, "Ariana, wake up. Something's coming. I'll get help."

Ariana almost jumped as she woke up. There was a crashing sound coming from the hairdressing salon. She used her thought magic to allow herself to see in the dark, as she pulled on her dressing gown, and walked down the hall, through the salon break room to the salon proper.

There she saw Jack, her ex-husband. She had not seen him since she saw him in court a month after their wedding. Paperwork had to be filed for a month before divorce proceedings could go ahead.

He was apparently trying to be sneaky, but had knocked over a potted plant.

"What do you want, Jack?" Ariana asked.

"I wanted to see you."

"In the middle of the night? By breaking in?"

"There's something I need. You're not going to understand it. I didn't know if it would go to you or your sister. But Martha's disappeared. I haven't seen her since the wedding. So I think you probably have it."

"So this something, what makes you think I have it?" Ariana wasn't afraid. Jack was just a man, he was no threat to a powerful witch.

"It was from one of your ancestors, would go down in the family line. I heard she died. So it either came to your sister or you."

Ariana began to realise that Jack was probably talking about Lady Arabella March. If that was the case, it was possible he knew something about magic. This was a little more concerning. "I don't know what you're talking about. Mum and Dad died in that accident shortly after the wedding. Surely you heard about that at the time. It was in the news. Uncle Fred's still alive and kicking."

"It wouldn't have gone to your uncle. It goes through the maternal line."

"Sorry, I've got nothing. No idea what you want."

"You probably aren't aware you even have it. There's a whole world you don't know about. You would have been carrying it around, not knowing. I know you're going to have trouble believing this, but magic exists. This ancestor's magic will probably have come down to you. It's a burden you're not prepared for. You'd be so far out of your depth. Let me take it from you."

"Let you take it from me?"

"Yes. I know you can't handle it. Honestly, Martha was the more magically inclined of the two of you. I tried to test her out and had her put a spell on you, but it failed. If she couldn't handle magic, you surely can't."

Well, that was it. Ariana said, "So you married me, in hopes of getting Lady Arabella's magic? You had an affair with my sister in case she inherited it. And you were behind that stupid wishing spell. Oh, Jack, I have some sad news for you. Yes, I inherited Lady Arabella's magic, after she tried to steal mine and I killed her, because my own magic was much stronger than hers. And now, you've broken into my work, my home, to try to steal from me. Someone's in way out of their depth, but it's not me."

114

As she spoke, a group of her friends stepped into the room, out of the Interim. Orsinius Wishlet was brandishing Excalibur. Lady Justice held her ancestral sword. Merlin and Benwyn were both holding wizard's staffs.

Ariana continued, "Oh, and I have friends, powerful friends. I suggest you run away now. When I said I killed Lady Arabella, I meant I helped subdue her. The final blow was by Lady Justice. Attempting to steal someone else's magic is a capital offence, after all."

Jack began to utter some kind of spell. With a thought Ariana stopped it in his throat.

He began to look panicked. He pulled a wand from his pocket. There was a flash of a sword and the wand fell in halves. Orsinius Wishlet, holding Excalibur, put himself between Ariana and her ex-husband.

Jack ran for the door. It was locked. He went to the window, and jumped out through the plate glass, then limped away.

"Are you unhurt, Miss Sutton?" Merlin asked.

"I'm fine. Thanks for coming everyone, and thanks for the warning Benwyn, but I can handle Jack."

"You know him best," Lady Justice said. "Should we take action to prevent him from coming back?"

Ariana sighed. "I don't think he'll be back, but it turns out, I didn't know him at all. I wish Martha had talked to me about him, instead of casting that spell. Maybe she would be alive now."

A brief silence followed, broken by Benwyn, who said, "He was not the danger I was warned you about. Something bigger is coming. I don't know what it is, but it is worse than a minor wizard. I was unable to put a form to what it was, but I had a sense of great power."

The friends looked at each other uneasily.

Impending Threat

"I will make coffee," Orsinius Wishlet said. Through his friendship with Ariana, he had learned the value of the mildly magical liquid.

The friends sat around the table of the hairdressing salon's break room. They were: Lady Justice; Merlin, the wizard; the wizard Benwyn, who was formerly a cat; the powerful witch Lady Ariana; and Orsinius, a wisp, a former thief, and now Guardian of Mythical Objects.

Ariana asked, "Benwyn, you said you'd foreseen something coming. Tell us everything you know."

They all looked toward the wizard, and his green eyes seemed to glow, as he told his story. "It began with dreams. For several nights I have dreamed that I was once more a cat. It was different, however. I was wearing a collar, which was magical. It was being used to control me. I was a slave. At first I thought perhaps the dream was the result of nerves, that I might anxious over the soon-to-be child."

"Soon-to-be child?" Ariana asked. "Are you and Claire expecting a baby?"

"Indeed we are. Claire is feeling unwell much of the time, which is why I have come alone."

"In Arabella March's things, I found a potion to cure morning sickness. I will make it for her. Merlin, I'll get you to check the recipe for me first, if you don't mind. I'd like a second opinion before I trust too much of her work."

"I am sure Claire would be very grateful. To continue my story, over the past week, the dreams have expanded. I have seen each of you, my friends, also wearing the same collars, also being slaves."

Lady Justice asked, "Can you describe this collar?"

"Indeed. It was gold with rubies studded on it. All of the collars looked the same."

Lady Justice held out her hand and a huge, ancient book, in a long-forgotten language appeared there.

She turned the pages. "Here it is," she said. "I thought the collars sounded familiar. One of my ancestors recorded dealing with an organisation which enslaved magical beings, and stole their power. This organisation, which called itself a word which translates to 'The Power' in modern English, used enchanted gold collars, encrusted with rubies. My ancestor destroyed the organisation and freed the prisoners, but was never certain she had caught every member of The Power."

Merlin said, thoughtfully, "Do any of you believe it is a coincidence that our friend Benwyn has had this dream, at the same time as Miss Sutton's former husband has tried to steal her power, albeit unaware how powerful she actually was?"

The others shook their heads.

Ariana said, "I'm having trouble getting my head around all of this. I've only just discovered Jack was part of the magical world, that he married me and had an affair with my sister, because he believed one of us would inherit Lady Arabella's power. If he really is part of this ancient group, surely he should have had a better plan than to break in here so clumsily."

"Perhaps," Lady Justice said, "but remember, he didn't know you were a witch. You didn't know that yourself, when you married him. He thought you had inherited this power without realising it, not that you'd inherited it and simply added it to your own natural power."

Ariana sighed loudly. "I know people talk about how horrible their exes are, but I think mine might be taking horrible to the extreme. I can't believe I was ever in love with him, or that I thought he was in love with me. Marrying him was a huge mistake."

Orsinius carefully put his coffee cup down on the table. He put his hand on Ariana's arm. "If you had not married him, you would not have been trapped in the Interim by that spell. You and I would never have met. I am glad you were married to him for that very short time. My life is better because you are my friend."

Ariana smiled at him. "Yes. My life is better, too. Stranger, often more dangerous, but definitely better for knowing you, for knowing all of you. OK. I guess we need to find where Jack has run off to. I think we need some kind of plan as well."

Merlin said, "I believe we need to be armed. Mr Wishlet, you should retain Excalibur. Lady Ariana, I suspect Lady Arabella left some entirely unsavoury things in that Realm you have inherited."

Ariana said, "Well, let's see what goodies of Lady Arabella's we can use.

She opened the door that usually lead from that room to her residence, but now the door opened to a strange realm between realities, where her ancestor Lady Arabella had stored all of her possessions.

"Be careful in here," she said. "Merlin and I have only catalogued about a quarter of this, and some of it is extremely nasty."

"These could be valuable in a fight," Merlin said, picking up a box of small stoppered vials. "You throw them at your enemy and the vial breaks and burns them."

"Sulphuric acid, is nasty stuff," Ariana agreed, "but there's a risk of splashing ourselves, or stepping in it in a fight. I agree we take it, but we need to be very careful handling it. How about this?" She held up a glass bottle with a swirling blue liquid in it. "This was supposed to make weapons stronger. I think we should pour it over both Excalibur and Lady Justice's sword, and whatever other weapons we can find in here to take with us. I think that cupboard," she pointed, "has swords, one of those spiked ball on a chain things and some knives."

"The spiked ball on a chain is called a morning star," Benwyn said. "Some of my father's soldiers were very adept at it. Whenever I tried, I just hit my own shins. They are difficult to use, if untrained."

"Let's skip the morning star," Ariana said.

Merlin was thoughtful, "Lady Arabella's snake, Worm, was not merely decoration, or a store for some of her power. It was also a powerful weapon. Perhaps it is time for you to create your own version of this."

"My own snake? I hadn't thought about it. I had a magical cat for a while, but I'm glad he's decided to be a wizard again."

"It does not have to be a snake," Merlin said. "But something of meaning to you, something you can carry with you."

"There is something," Ariana said, and she held out her hand. A gold brooch, shaped like a butterfly dropped from the Interim into her hand. "This was my mother's."

"A butterfly? That is not an intimidating weapon like Lady Arabella's snake," Orsinius observed.

The others said nothing, but the way they looked at the object showed they agreed with Orsinius.

"None of you watch tv very much, do you?" Ariana said.

Apart from Ariana, the only member of the group to have watched television was Lady Justice, who had tried for sixteen years to give her daughter a normal, human, life.

Ariana continued, "I learned this from the great philosopher Bart Simpson: 'No-one suspects the butterfly.' I don't know how Lady Arabella did this, but I'm pretty sure I can just do it with my thought magic."

119

She held the butterfly and concentrated. Then she released it and it flew to attach itself to her blouse.

Benwyn selected a sword, and treated it with the blue swirling potion, then he hid it in his robes. He also held his wizard's staff. Merlin followed Benwyn's lead and similarly hid a treated sword.

They returned through the door, to the break room.

"To find Jack, I guess I need to do some scrying," Ariana said.

"Do you have something you received from him?" Merlin asked.

Ariana held out her hand, and a gold ring fell out of the Interim into her hand. "Wedding ring," she said.

She opened the maps app on her phone, and sat the ring on the screen. The map began to move.

They watched, until the map settled in position under the ring.

"He didn't go far," Ariana said.

"Are we ready?" Merlin asked.

"I'll take us," Ariana said. She looked at the map, and thought them all to the street outside the address shown.

Butterfly Spy

Orsinius, Ariana, Lady Justice, Merlin and Benwyn stood on the footpath in front of the old house.

Ariana provided a glamour so passers-by would not see or hear them.

"I think we need to know what's happening inside," Ariana said. A gold butterfly brooch pinned on her blouse tentatively tested its wings, then flew over the fence, through the front yard, and in through a partly-open window.

Ariana held out her hand, and a ball of mist formed, hovering over her palm. In the mist they could observe what the butterfly could see.

The butterfly had found itself a vantage point on top of a curtain rod. From there, the watchers outside could look down on Jack, as he paced around the lounge room, talking on his phone.

"I told you, it's impossible," he said. "She's not some unknowing innocent. She's a witch, and she knows how to use that power... Well, no, when I married her, I was sure she didn't know... wasn't aware of magic... It's been a while... And she had friends who just stepped out of the Interim... No. No. Listen to me. One of her friends was Lady Justice! ... And I let it slip I was behind the spell her sister used against her, and now Lady Justice knows. I am going to die... And I didn't get Lady Arabella's power, but... You're not listening. Ariana has her own power as well as Lady Arabella's, and she was powerful enough to beat Lady Arabella... No! No! I'm out! If I'm going to get away from Lady Justice, I have to run now! I don't even know where I can hide... So no, no, I didn't get the power from Ariana, I couldn't get it, and I doubt anyone else in The Power could get it either... Yes, I'm a coward. I'll accept that. You fight them if you want to. You're the great and powerful wizard. We all know I'm not much of a practitioner of any kind. No, I'm not being your errand-boy any more. I'm leaving the country. I wish I could leave the planet…"

Outside Ariana said, "I think he's avoiding you, Lady J."

Lady Justice smiled and said, "You'd be surprised how many people don't want a visit from me."

Benwyn said, "He's clearly only a minor part of this organisation."

"Definitely not the brains of the operation," Ariana said. "How did I ever overlook what a spineless, simpering, idiot he was?"

Merlin said, "But back then, Miss Sutton, you did not know how powerful you were, and had not experienced the adventures you've had. You have continued to grow and learn. It does not appear your ex-husband did either of those things."

Orsinius asked the group, "What do we do now? Should we capture him, and demand information about The Power and its plans?"

Lady Justice said, "I do have an obligation to seperate his head from his shoulders, given he has admitted to being part of a malicious misuse of magic. Perhaps we could offer him a slight extension of time to live, in return for information."

"I wonder if that was his own idea, or if The Power was behind that, too," Ariana mused.

"It's certainly more complicated that it appeared at the time," Lady Justice said.

"I believe we should enter the house. I doubt Mr Jones will give us much of a fight," Merlin said.

Ariana waved her hand, and the five of them appeared in the lounge room, in front of Jack. In his yelling and pacing, he almost walked into them before realising they were there. He screamed, a high pitched shriek which sounded far too feminine for him, and dropped the phone.

Orsinius picked up the phone and offered it to Lady Justice.

Lady Justice spoke into the phone, "Hello, this is Lady Justice, to whom am I speaking? … They hung up. How rude of them! I suppose Jack Jones is going to have to give us information after all."

She drew her scimitar from its hiding place under her left wing. Ariana was always amazed Lady Justice didn't cut off her own wings with the manoeuvre.

Jack turned pale, and began to shake. "No! No! Please! I haven't done anything!"

Lady Justice replied, "Not done anything? Yet, at Ariana's home, I overheard you telling her that you were behind the spell that trapped her in the Interim. I've already executed your co-conspirator in that crime. I also heard that you were there to steal her power, the power she inherited, of course, not her own natural power that you were unaware of. So I have more than enough evidence to pass judgement. I may be willing to negotiate a brief reprieve for you to get your affairs in order, if you co-operate with my current investigation of The Power."

"Ah, no. No. It's not that I don't want to help, but they will kill me."

"I will kill you."

Jack turned to Ariana, "Please, Ariana, I'm begging you, help me. I'm sorry for everything. I never meant to hurt you."

Ariana's voice was hard as she said, "You never meant to hurt me. Yet you cheated on me with my sister, and tried to kill me. Tell me, what exactly did you mean to do?"

Jack sat down, his head in his hands. Tears poured down his face as he sniffed. His ex-wife and her friends simply stood, staring down at him.

Finally, through audible sobs, he said, "What do you want to know?

The Power

The five friends: the wizards Merlin and Benwyn; Lady Justice, the witch Lady Ariana, and Orsinius Wishlet, a wisp and Guardian of Mythical Objects; gathered around Jack Jones, as he sat, head in hands. "The Power isn't really an organisation. It's just one person, who pretends to have a massive group of people following him. His name is…"

Jack collapsed on the floor, grabbing at his neck as he struggled to breathe.

Ariana waved her hand over him, and revealed a gold collar, studded with rubies, that had been covered by a glamour. She grabbed the collar, and it crumbled to dust in her hand.

"How long have you been controlled like this?" Ariana asked.

"Five years, since just before I met you," Jack answered. "I really am sorry. I didn't have any choice in how I treated you."

Lady Justice asked, "Who is he?"

Jack, rubbing his bruised neck said, "His name is…"

There was a flash of light and another wizard appeared in the room.

"Mordred!" Merlin exclaimed.

The new wizard looked at Merlin and said, "Hey Merlin. Long time no see. Not long enough, obviously. Oh, and look, Excalibur's here as well. Any more old friends I should be aware of?"

Lady Justice asked, "You enslaved this man?"

"'Enslaved' is such a harsh word. I sought his assistance, shall we say?"

"You 'sought his assistance' using one of the gold collars The Power used to use?"

"Well, way back in the dark ages, I was part of the group. I wasn't a big part of it, but I was working my way up. I got involved to have them help me destroy Arthur. Merlin knows the story, or some of it. It was just politics, nothing bad. But then your ancestor came along and killed everyone else. She left the collars they used. So I took them, figured they'd come in handy. Anyway, if you're going to ask me more questions, I think I want legal representation."

"You're entitled to call on a solicitor if you wish."

Mordred called the name "Corvin Ravenwing" three times, and the bird known by that name flew out of the Interim and in through the same window as Ariana's butterfly had done earlier.

"Hi Corvin," Ariana said.

The raven bowed and said, "Good morning, Lady Ariana."

"Lady Ariana?" Jack asked.

Corvin answered, "Lady Ariana inherited the title along with everything else a wealthy ancestor left her."

Corvin then bowed to each of the beings present and greeted them accordingly.

"Do I get time to consult my legal counsel in private?" Mordred asked.

"That is acceptable," Lady Justice said.

Mordred led Corvin to another room.

The friends and Jack waited.

Ariana handed her wedding ring to Jack, and said, "I meant to give this back to you when we went to court for the divorce, but in the stress of the moment, I left it behind.

Before Jack could answer, they heard Corvin's voice yelling: "No!"

Orsinius and Ariana were first to rush to the room, where they found Corvin on the floor, struggling with a gold collar around his neck.

Ariana crushed the collar as she had done the previous one.

"He was going to use me to try to steal your power," Corvin gasped.

"Which way did he go?" Ariana asked.

"The window, then he disappeared into the Interim."

"The time difference in the Interim means he could be anywhere by now," Ariana said, sadly.

She and Orsinius helped Corvin back to the others.

"What do we do now?" Ariana asked.

"We ask Excalibur," Merlin answered.

"We what?" Ariana was confused.

"Excalibur will remember Mordred, because Excalibur belonged to, and was loyal to Arthur. It won't have forgotten Mordred's treachery. Excalibur, please take us to Mordred."

Orsinius felt the sword pulling in his hand, leading him into the Interim. The wizards, Lady Justice and Ariana followed, leaving Corvin and Jack alone.

When Orsinius and those following him exited the Interim, they appeared to be in a cave. Following Excalibur, they found Mordred deep in the cave, in an area that appeared to be used as a storeroom. On a shelf, were six gold collars, studded with rubies, similar to the two Ariana had already destroyed.

Ariana picked up each in turn, and turned them to dust. Then the group turned to Mordred, who was cowering in a corner.

"Using magic to enslave people, and birds, is a malicious misuse of magic," Lady Justice said. "I believe your attack on your legal counsel is such a grievous act that you may no longer have representation. Is there anything you wish to say before I enact judgment?"

Mordred shook his head.

Lady Justice promptly removed that head.

Ariana thought them all back to Jack's lounge room, where Lady Justice granted Jack a stay of execution for crimes committed while he was compelled to act on Mordred's orders, on the strict condition of good behaviour going forward.

Corvin bowed to Ariana and thanked her for saving his life. He promised to represent her for any and all future magical legal matters free. Ariana thanked him, but said any repayment was unnecessary. She was glad to help a friend.

Reflections

Final notes on the case of Mordred and The Power, A.D. 2023. Relates to the case *In Virtute* conducted by Theophena, the eight hundred and thirty-second Lady Justice. Also relates to my own case of Martha Sutton, and to the case of Jack Jones.

I have already recorded details of the event of the case, and my decision to execute the wizard Mordred in accordance with established magical law and lore.

With this further note, I would like to give my own observations.

We do not know why Mordred chose to present himself to myself and my associates when Jack Jones was released from his power. It is entirely feasible that, had he not done so, he may have been able to escape. I suspect it was a matter of pride or ego, that he believed we should know who he was.

Merlin has suggested another, far more insidious, possibility, that I cannot exclude: that Mordred was not, in fact, the only member of *In Virtute*/The Power, and that he sacrificed himself to protect other members. This would likely mean that the gold collars Lady Ariana Sutton destroyed were not all of the collars in existence. If Merlin is correct, that may mean we have not heard the last of this organisation.

In the light of current information, I have not imposed penalty on Jack Jones for his crimes, in attempting to steal power from Lady Ariana, and in encouraging Martha Sutton to trap Lady Ariana in the Interim. Despite this, I still believe the execution of Miss Martha Sutton for the misuse of magic was appropriate. Although influenced by Mr Jones, Miss Sutton knew what she was doing to Lady Ariana was wrong.

I wish to record the following commendations of my associates in this matter:

Lady Ariana is the most powerful witch known to exist at this, or any time. Although coming to magic relatively late in life, she has managed to continue to maintain control of her own power, and has remained humble, and determined to do good. With the power to do anything, she prefers to work at hairdressing, and that people not use her title.

The Great Wizard Merlin, who is, as he has always been, a powerful force for good, and a keen tutor to those learning the ways of magic. No-one, not even Merlin himself, knows his age and how long he has been providing such great service to the magical community, however our records have mentioned him more than five thousand years in the past.

Lord Benwyn of Canterbury, who inherited his title five hundred years ago, and who has suffered centuries of self-imposed penalty for his own guilty conscience, has proved a great benefit to the cause of magical justice, both now as a wizard, and in the past, as a cat. This case could not have been successful without his foresight.

Finally, there is Orsinius Wishlet, who for so many years was a nuisance petty criminal, a thief who would use the Interim to steal from humans. Most of the thefts were of minor items that no-one would miss. I have seen his burrow, and his number of small thefts must have been in the hundreds of thousands. Some years ago, Merlin told me that he saw a great potential in Mr Wishlet. At the time I was unable to see anything of value in him at all. I have never been more pleased to be proved completely wrong. Mr Wishlet went from being a petty criminal to, with the help of Lady Ariana, living an honest life in the human world, and then on to become the Guardian of Mythical Objects, a role in which he has never disappointed us. At times I wonder what Mr Wishlet's life would have been had he not met Lady Ariana, but I realise that would have been an entirely different story.

In my reign as the current Lady Justice I have had many firsts: I have been the first to use imprisonment instead of execution as a penalty. I have been the first to offer parole. I have been the first to grant clemency to an offender who had been operating under the control of another, and I have been the first to have have worked with a group people who are determined to assist with the ends of justice.

I hope future generations will see these things as improvements to the way things have been done before, and will build on them, to the betterment of magical justice.

Ariadne,

Nine hundred and fifty-sixth Lady Justice.

Potion

Augustus Wishlet was rearranging the odious items on the shelves in his dingy shop, when a man entered through the sliding bookshelf that linked "real" shop to the unassuming bookshop in front of it.

"Good morning sir, may I help you with something?" Augustus said in his most professional customer-service voice. He had learned this from his more recent encounters with his cousin Orsinius, who worked in a hairdressing salon.

"Yes," the tall, very pale, man said. "I heard you were able to get obscure items."

"Almost always. What are you after, in particular?"

"I want a love potion, not one of those mass-produced fakes, but a real one, specific to a particular couple."

"Those are hard to source, but I may know someone who can create one."

In truth, Augustus did know someone who would be able to create one, the witch Ariana, was the hairdresser his cousin worked for. She definitely had the ability to do it. Whether she would be convinced to do so or not, was another matter.

"I understand you would need items that link the two people," the customer said. He handed Augustus two gold rings. "These were our wedding rings. I re-acquired hers recently. I want my ex-wife back. I made some mistakes, but I'm sure I could do better if she gave me a chance."

"If I can get this done, it will be very expensive."

"I don't care about the cost." Once he had access to his ex-wife's inheritance, he was certain he could afford to pay anything.

Augustus pocketed the rings. "Come back tomorrow. I will know by then if I can help you."

The customer exited the way he had come.

Augustus locked the door behind him, then slipped into the Interim, emerging in Ariana's hairdressing salon.

It was the end of the working day. Orsinius was sweeping the floor. Andy Justice, the apprentice, was stacking used scissors, combs, and other equipment in a sterilising machine. Ariana was working on the salon's books.

Augustus was somewhat anxious. Even his cousin, whom he had bullied for most of his life, was now someone far more powerful than him.

"Excuse me, Lady Ariana. I would like to ask a favour," Augustus said. He noticed that all three had stopped working to look at him.

"Hello Augustus. What can I do for you?" Ariana answered.

"A customer asked for a love potion, a real one, that will actually work. You are the only being I know who is powerful enough to produce one."

"I don't like the idea of love potions. Taking away someone's choice seems to me to be wrong. You can't force someone to love you," Ariana said.

"It's also illegal," Andy said. "Several of my ancestors executed people for making them. Taking away people's freedom of choice is a breach of magical law."

Of course Lady Justice's daughter would know that, Augustus thought.

Augustus took the rings from his pocket and put them on the counter beside Ariana. "Can you do anything with these, at all? Anything that might at least look like a love potion? If people hear I couldn't provide what a customer wanted, they will stop buying from me."

Ariana looked at the rings, picked them up, and looked closer. She asked, "Where did you get these?"

"From my customer. You need something to link the two people, for the potion, do you not?"

"Right," Ariana said, "I'll give him a potion."

She opened a door and entered an alternate realm. Half an hour later, she was back. She gave Augustus a small jar in which the two rings were submerged in a deep red liquid.

She said. "Tell him he needs to go home and run a bath. He's to put both rings on, pour the liquid into the bath, and soak for at least half an hour. Don't tell him who created the potion before he uses it. If he comes back later to ask questions, you can give in and tell him."

Augustus bowed low, thanked Ariana profusely, and re-entered the Interim.

"Love potions are illegal," Andy said. "My Mum's not going to be happy about this."

"It isn't a love potion," Ariana answered.

"You knew those rings, I saw on your face." Orsinius said. He had known his friend for some time now, and recognised her angry reaction to the rings.

"They were Jack's and my wedding rings. I gave him back mine after I used it to scry for him that time. I'm guessing he thought he could still take advantage of my abilities, even after that debacle with Mordred."

Andy asked, "So what's that potion? What will happen when he puts the ring on?"

Ariana smiled. "There's no potion, and nothing illegal. It's just hair dye. I guess he's going to get caught red-handed, and red everything else as well, trying to manipulate me."

Andy asked, "Are you going to tell him it was only dye? I mean, if he comes to you and asks?"

Ariana thought a moment, and answered, "I might tell him eventually. I'd like him to wonder for a while."

Narcissus

Ariana was cutting Lady Justice's hair when he walked into the salon. Her ex-husband Jack was red from head to toe. Ariana stifled her laughter.

Jack said, "Can we talk for a minute?"

Ariana replied, "You can see I'm busy. Anything you want to say to me, you can say in front of my friends."

Jack answered, "But don't you want to see me alone?"

"Not particularly."

"But you must."

"Because you bought a love potion?"

"How did you know?"

Orsinius Wishlet and Andy Justice were listening to the conversation from the break room, trying not to laugh.

"So you didn't even go back to Augustus, and ask questions, when you found out the potion was a dye."

"When what?"

"I thought you'd go back to Augustus, who would tell you he came to me, and I wouldn't make the potion, because love potions are illegal, and I wouldn't make one for you anyway."

"But he gave me a potion, and it did something."

"It changed the colour of your skin. Bathing in hair dye, especially permanent hair dye, will do that."

Now none of her friends were hiding their laughter. Andy and Orsinius came into the main room of the salon to watch, as well as listen to, the entertainment.

Ariana continued, "Besides, you really wouldn't want me to make you a love potion. It would have made the owners of both of those rings obsessed with each other. And you were

135

just trying to get me to fall for you, so you could influence me to give you my power. You didn't want it to be reciprocal. You may as well take those rings off. You didn't get what you wanted."

Jack looked down at the two gold rings on his left hand. "Our wedding rings don't mean anything to you anymore?"

"Let's see. You cheated on me with my sister, and persuaded her to try to kill me. You tried to trick me into giving you my power. You only married me because you'd joined a secret society, that then enslaved you to make you try to steal my power. So our whole relationship was built on a lie. Then you tried to acquire a love potion to manipulate me. Yeah, those rings mean something. They mean the biggest mistake of my life is in the past."

"But, we could start over, if the potion had worked. You once thought we belonged together. I still think we do. I've messed things up, but I'm ready to change."

"What do you mean you 'still think we do'? You never thought anything of the sort. You didn't choose to be in a relationship with me, your puppet master did. You really think a love potion was the solution to the mess you've made of your life?"

"Yes?" It was hesitant, more a question than a statement.

"OK. Instead of a potion. I'll just do the magic directly on the rings. Give them to me, I will make it so the owners of both are madly in love with each other. You're sure you consent to this?"

"Of course, I consent."

"Lady Justice, this is legal, if the subject consents, isn't it?"

Lady Justice said, "It's legal, but it's not advisable. This man is not someone you want to be in a relationship with."

Ariana smiled. "Jack, I have to ask you again. You're sure about this?"

"Yes, I'm sure."

He handed her the rings. She held them a moment, then gave them back and told him to put both on again.

Jack held the rings in his hand a moment, then put them back on. He looked into a salon mirror, transfixed.

"Those rings are both yours, Jack," Ariana said. "I gave you one when we were married, and I gave the other one back to you more recently. You're now obsessed with the person you were in love with all along. I'll remind you, you not only requested this but consented to it, when I asked you twice."

Jack ignored her.

"Jack, you've always been a narcissist, so now you're sharing the fate of Narcissus. I'm sending you home now."

Ariana made a dismissive motion with her hand and Jack vanished.

"You can't leave him like that," Lady Justice said.

"I thought I'd leave it a couple of hours," Ariana answered, "to give him time to realise how stupid he's being. When I release him from that, though, I need a way to get him to leave me alone permanently. Does the magical justice system have restraining orders?"

"It hasn't before, but I've made so many innovations lately, and this makes sense, so I'll grant it. Release him in two hours, and I will go and explain to him that if he harasses you again, he's losing his head. I've already let him off so much more than any of my ancestors would have, because of his circumstances."

Bear Essentials

The sign on the small shop said, "Bear Essentials" and the window display was full of bears of all kinds.

Inside the shop, shelves were filled with bears. There were no other types of toys in the shop, only plush bears. There were pink bears and blue bears. There were yellow, brown, and white bears. There were bears with bows and bears with clothes. There were bears as big as a child, and tiny bears which would fit in a little dolls' house.

In one corner, bears were having a teddy-bears picnic. In another a huge bear was reading Winnie the Pooh. On the counter beside the cash register was a smallish, very worn, bear, with a small sign saying, "Not for Sale", as if anyone would want to buy such a bear with all the other magnificent bears on display.

Behind the counter sat Cara. She was the owner and only worker in the shop. Cara drank coffee and read a book, occasionally saying something, appearing to talk to herself.

The bell over the door rang, as a woman and a small girl entered the shop. The woman was saying, "We're just looking, not buying, and we look with our eyes, not our fingers."

Cara smiled. "Hello," she said. "Let me know if I can help you, or if you want to know anything about the bears."

The young mother, nodded, and said, "Thank you, we're just looking."

Cara noticed the mother and child both had worn clothing. At least the child's was second-hand, perhaps the mother's was too, although they could just have been very old. The clothes were clean and well-cared for, but old.

The little girl looked, wide-eyed at all the magnificent bears on display. She squealed with delight at the teddy-bear's picnic. She chattered to her mother about the book the big bear was reading, and asked if they could find it in the library. Cara noticed she kept her hands behind her back so she wouldn't be tempted to touch.

Then she saw the old bear on the counter. "Excuse me," the girl said, "but why does that bear look like that?"

Cara smiled. "This is my own bear," she said. "Bear and I have been best friends since I was a little girl. When bears are loved a very long time they start to look a little ragged, but they are still beautiful, don't you think?"

The girl looked at the bear. "Yes," she said as if she'd just made a firm decision. "A loved bear looks lovely."

"Oh, I think so," Cara answered.

"That bear looks especially lovely too," the girl said, and pointed to a bear on the shelf behind the counter. It was a handcrafted, one-of-a-kind by highly respected toymaker. She sighed, "I wish I could have a bear like that."

"Would you like a closer look?" Cara asked. As she took the bear down from the shelf, she tore the price tag, removing "00.00" from the end of the price. She placed the bear on the counter, where the girl could look at it more closely.

"It's so beautiful," the girl said with absolute awe. "It's the most beautiful bear I have ever seen."

Cara looked at the mother. "Just for today, it's on sale for five dollars," she said.

The mother looked confused at first. She had seen other prices, and realised the bear could not be worth so little. "Did you say five dollars?" she asked.

Cara smiled at her. "Yes, five dollars."

The mother paid the five dollars. The small girl had a massive smile as she skipped out of the store with her new bear. As the door closed behind them, the bell rang again.

"You're a terrible businesswoman," the worn bear on the counter said.

"I know," Cara answered.

"You'll never make a profit doing things like that," Bear said.

"No, I won't, but I will make children happy, and bears will be loved."

"Well, I personally don't need to eat, so it really doesn't bother me, but you need to think about the realities of life."

"When I was little, my parents would never have been able to afford a bear as magnificent as you. My mother used to spend a lot of time with an elderly neighbour who was lonely. That neighbour gave you to me. Customers will come who can afford the more expensive bears, but very few of the bears they buy will be as loved as that one will be, or as you are."

Betsy's Books

Elizabeth exited the bus at the stop on the corner of Main Street and Lilly Pilly Lane.

Lilly Pilly Lane was not the narrow, dismal side street the term "lane" usually implied. Instead it was a wide avenue. In the centre was a traffic island, with tall lilly pilly trees growing. The trees had their early spring growth, new leaves bursting out in red and orange colours. Soon the leaves would settle to the normal green, and puffy mauve flowers would emerge, to later be replaced by ripe colourful fruit. Under the trees, the traffic island was covered in creeping native flowers, in many bright colours. At each end of the lane, and in the middle, there was a break in the traffic island, to allow for pedestrian crossings. At each side of the road, there was plenty of parking available, as well as another free car park around the corner at the other end of the lane.

The footpaths on either side were paved with terracotta tiles. Fronting on to these footpaths were charming small shops, all with old-fashioned awnings that covered the footpath, to make the space cool and pleasant for shoppers.

This shopping district had been a special project of the city council, to create a pleasant and unique shopping experience, and revitalise a part of the city that had fallen into disrepair.

She stopped at the coffee shop, and bought three coffees: two cappuccinos and a long black.

Continuing on her way, she stopped again at Bear Essentials. She gave a cappuccino to Cara, who was opening up the shop. The two women chatted for a short while, and Elizabeth chose a bear for her niece's birthday. She paid, and asked Cara to hold it until the end of the day for Elizabeth to collect on her way home.

Next door to Bear Essentials was Betsy's Books. In front of the shop, Carlton was already sitting on his folding chair, with copies of The Big Issue stacked on the footpath beside him.

Elizabeth handed the black coffee to Carlton.

He took it and smiled. "Black as pitch, unsweetened, and hot, exactly how I like it," he said, and smiled, showing his severe shortage of teeth. "Thank you gracious lady."

"You're welcome," Elizabeth said. "Is that the new issue?"

"Nah," he answered. "You've got this one already. When I get the new one, you'll be the first person I tell."

"Thanks. Have a good day," Elizabeth said, as she unlocked the door and walked inside. She turned the sign from "closed" to "open" and prepared for her morning routine.

She turned on the lights, and the cash register, and logged in to her card reading machine. In the corner reading nook, she picked up the books from the small table and returned them to the second-hand book shelves, getting out others that might appeal to a general audience, and put those on the tables instead. She did the same with the books placed in the children's reading corner. Each day, there were different books out in the two reading areas. Shoppers could stop and read, and decide if they wanted to buy.

In the other section of the shop, she took the book on the "featured" display in the local authors' section, put it back in the shelf, and got out another book to feature for the day.

Her business was in two clear parts. In one section of the shop, she bought and sold second-hand books, with pricing based on the condition, rarity, and quality, of the books. Usually she charged ten percent more for the books than the price she paid for them. The other section was books taken on consignment from local independent authors. Those books were new and charged at full price. Once they were sold, she would keep ten percent of the price, and pay the rest to the author. At the end of each month, she sent each author an account of which of their books had sold, and how much she was paying, and she sent their payments electronically.

A young man entered the shop.

"I'm looking for a book," he said.

"Good morning," Elizabeth replied. "Well, you're in the right place. What kind of book do you want?"

"It's for my girlfriend," he said.

"What does your girlfriend normally read?"

"Books."

"Do you know what authors she likes? What genres?"

"What what?"

"Writers, types of stories. Does she like romance, or vampires, or mysteries?"

"I don't know. She's reading one that's red, and the last one was black."

"All one colour? Like leather bindings? Hard covers, with leather over the cover?"

"Really old."

"Right. There's classics over in this shelf. They're old, but still great stories. Some of them are even leather bound."

"How do I know which one to get?"

"Do you have much time?"

"A bit. Why?"

"Take a couple of books, and go and sit on the comfy couch in the reading corner. Read the first two or three pages of each book, then decide which one seems like something your girlfriend would like."

The customer took six books to the reading corner, and began to studiously read the beginning of each.

A young mother, with a toddler entered the shop. "Hi," she said.

"Good morning," Elizabeth replied. "How can I help you today?"

"I'm looking for kids' picture books. We're getting bored with the ones at the library, and most of the big bookshops just seem to have the same ones as the library has."

"Well, in our second-hand section we have some kids books that you might not have seen, but more exciting, one of our local indie authors writes and illustrates books about native animals."

Elizabeth showed the mother where to find both the second-hand children's books, and the ones by local authors, she also showed them the children's reading area, in case they wanted to look at the books before buying.

With her customers happily browsing, Elizabeth went back to her seat behind the counter, to continue reading her own book.

A man in a business suit entered. Without greeting Elizabeth, he said, "You've got a homeless guy set up shop outside."

"You mean my friend, Carlton? Yes, that's his usual spot."

"Your friend? It's not a good look for a business to have people like that hanging around."

"My business does well enough, with Carlton there."

The man made a grunting noise and stalked off to look at the second-hand books. He came back and said, "These are all over-priced. I could get the same books for free from those street library things."

"Then I encourage you to do that," Elizabeth said, trying to keep her anger at this obnoxious man under control.

He made another grunting noise, then went to the consignment section. From there, he called out: "These books are outrageously priced!"

Not wanting to yell across the shop, Elizabeth walked over to him. "Those are new books," she said. "That's what new books cost."

"You're pricing yourself out of business," he said.

"As I said before, my business is fine. People who appreciate books, and know their value, are more than happy to buy them."

The young mother, and her toddler approached the counter, with a pile of books, both new and used.

Elizabeth excused herself from the abrasive man and went to check them out.

"You're far more patient than I would be," the woman whispered to Elizabeth.

"It's not my first rodeo," Elizabeth answered. "Enjoy your books, and please come back when you want more."

The woman smiled and thanked her, and the toddler, half-hiding behind her mother's legs waved shyly.

As they left, a woman with pink hair entered. She was a regular customer, who worked in one of the shops in Lilly Pilly Lane.

The woman placed a bag of used books on the counter. "Hi Bets," she said. "Just take it off the books I'm buying today."

She went on to browse the shelves, while Elizabeth took out the books, and calculated what she was willing to pay for them.

Carlton entered. "Hey beautiful lady," he said. "Just leaving my stuff here while I get lunch. Want me to pick yours up?"

"Where are you going?"

"The bakery."

"Awesome. Just a salad roll for me, thanks. Keep the change."

She took a twenty out of her handbag, knowing her lunch would cost about ten.

The man in the business suit grunted again. He walked over to the counter after Carlton left.

"That homeless man acts like he belongs. You let people just sit and read all day, and you don't even know if they're buying anything, and what's with the woman with the weird hair? Is that your standard of regular customer? You just let anyone in here?"

Elizabeth smiled as sweetly as she could, "Yes, I do let anyone in here. I even let you in."

"I was thinking of making an offer to buy this business, but the way it's been run, it would take too much work to fix it."

"That's OK. It was never for sale anyway."

"Maybe I'll just find out who your landlord is and buy the building."

"No need to find out. I'm my own landlord. I'm not selling the building either. I think you'll find that none of the businesses in the lane will suit you. We all have pretty much the same culture."

The man grunted once more as he walked out.

The woman with the pink hair came to the counter with an armload of books. She said, "Well, he was charming. You should have mentioned you're chair of the Lilly Pilly Lane Business Association. Maybe that would scare him off trying with anyone else."

"I don't think it would. That man was too sure of his own superiority for anything to make a difference to him."

146

"I'll put the word out for everyone to look out for him. Did he just walk into Bear Essentials?"

Elizabeth grinned, and said, "Cara's going to have fun with him. I wonder if she'll try the ventriloquist thing of hers where it sounds like the old bear beside the register's talking?"

"You sure that's ventriloquism? I kind of thought the bear might be possessed or something."

"Cara would say it's been made real with love, like the Velveteen Rabbit."

The woman paid for her books. She was still there when the young man came to the counter with all of the books he'd taken to read.

"I'm getting all of them," he said. "This one's for my girlfriend, but I want the others. I didn't know books were so cool. And you'll buy them back from me when I've finished reading them, and come back to buy more?"

"That's the way it works," Elizabeth confirmed. "Unless you want to keep them."

"Cool. That bloke that just left was a bit over the top wasn't he?"

"More than a bit," the woman with the pink hair said. "My boss would have just kicked him out if he'd come in and tried to tell her how to run her business."

They heard a yell from the next shop, then the door slammed.

"The bear," the pink-haired woman said.

"Yup, pretty sure of," Elizabeth answered as she started checking out the young man's books.

"So, what's the story of the bear?" the young man asked.

"Come with me," the woman with the pink hair said, "I'll introduce you to Cara and her bear."

As they left, Carlton returned with lunch.

147

"Let's eat over in the reading corner," Elizabeth said. "I think I'm closing the shop for half an hour. It's been a busy morning."

"When I was walking back," Carlton said, "I saw that stuck up guy in the suit fly out of Cara's shop and take off up the street like a scared rabbit. What's that about."

"It's about a stuck up guy in a suit thinking he knows everything, and can have anything."

"They usually do," Carlton said.

Crafty Capers

On Wednesday mornings, the knitting circle met at Crafty Capers. The activity didn't directly make any money, but the knitters tended to buy their yarn there. Andrea was happy to have the ladies take over the corner of her shop for the morning.

There was something soothing about the click click click of needles and the women's voices chatting. The four regulars were here, the eighty year old twins Enid and Edna, who had spent a hard life on the family farm before moving to a retirement village, the retired teacher Mavis, and housewife Ivy. A fifth member had recently joined the group, Shelley, who was able to come in breaks between uni lectures. The older ladies were teaching her.

This was one group Andrea didn't have to actively supervise. The ladies just enjoyed sitting together knitting their own projects.

Andrea was able to continue on with her work, tidying and stocking shelves, writing orders and suchlike. She would occasionally join the ladies for a couple of minutes and chat.

She enjoyed having the knitters there. The elderly ladies reminded her of her grandmother, and the clicking of the knitting needles reminded her of evenings sitting beside her grandmother, watching yarn magically turn into garments.

Watching the older women teach Shelley, patiently showing her how to do the different stitches, made Andrea think of the way her grandmother had patiently taught her.

Customers came and went throughout the morning.

Carlton stopped by and said, "I'm heading to the bakery to pick up lunch for Bet and me. You want anything?"

Andrea went to her handbag, behind the counter. She got a twenty dollar note and handed it to Carlton. "Can you get me a sausage roll, with tomato sauce, and a diet cola. Keep the change."

She realised that Elizabeth would have also given him extra for her food. It was a thing the business owners did to help ensure the homeless man had at least one real meal per day. He'd always offer to pick up lunch for at least two of them, and each would give him double the amount their lunch would cost.

Carlton left to go to the bakery.

A tall, gaunt woman entered. She started searching shelves, picking things up, putting things down.

Andrea asked, "Can I help you?"

The woman waved her away, without saying anything.

Over in the corner, one of the knitters said, "Rude," just loudly enough that everyone in the shop heard it.

The thin woman had found her way to the drawers of raw fibre.

"Tell me about the alpaca fleece," the woman said abruptly.

"What do you want to know?" Andrea said, "The alpacas' names are Geoffrey and Isabel."

"You know their names?" The woman seemed surprised.

"And the merino fleece comes from Louise and Mary. They all belong to Pete's Petting Zoo. I buy their fleece every year. So I don't have a lot, but I don't have a lot of customers who spin their own yarn."

"It's always a party with Pete's," Shelley said from the corner where the knitters were sitting.

Andrea smiled, "You've seen his ads?"

"Nah, he came to my little brother's birthday party. I met all those animals you get fleece from. I'd love to be able to spin yarn to knit. But I guess I've got to learn to knit properly first."

"You'll get there," Edna said. "It just takes practice."

"I'll take all your alpaca fleece, and the merino as well," the thin customer said. "How long before you get more in?"

"At the end of winter or beginning of spring. Shearing only happens once a year."

Andrea wrapped the fleece in paper, and checked the customer out.

Carlton dropped Andrea's lunch back. Andrea went to sit with the knitters while she ate. She joined in their conversation for a while. Eventually, the knitters packed up to leave. Edna and Elsie both bought more yarn. The group went were going to the coffee shop after their meeting.

Andrea set up the big table and the chairs for the after school craft class. She gathered together collage equipment, and spread it along the centre of the table, trying to ensure each kid would be able to reach some of each item. This week it was collage, next week paper quilling.

She loved the after school craft group. She tried to give the kids something different each week. It reminded her of all the amazing craft activities that, as a child, she'd done with her grandmother.

Andrea looked around her shop. Everything seemed to be filled with memories of her grandmother, and the things they did together.

Bouncing Bean

Practically everyone who ever shops or works in Lilly Pilly Lane stops for coffee at the Bouncing Bean.

People like the coffee beans painted on the walls, the cute little white tables and chairs, and the outside seating on the footpath under the shade of the wide awnings. Most of all they like, the expertly-made coffee and other beverages, along with the biscuits, cakes and other sweet treats.

The Bouncing Bean is owned and operated by Sharon, who is assisted by Jasmine. These very professional and competent baristas are known by other people who work in the Lane as the Odd Couple. Sharon stands tall and straight. Her long brown hair is always swept up and pinned firmly in place, and wears lacy blouses and linen skirts, with high heels. Jas has short spiked hair, which is currently vibrant blue, but can be any colour on any day, and wears tee shirts, torn jeans, and Doc Martens boots, some times she wears her hair black, and teams it up with heavy black eyeliner to go full-on goth.

On this day, Sharon opened the shop at seven in the morning. She served most of the shop owners and their staff with coffee on their way to work. Then the early shoppers came by for morning tea, or to grab a quick take away cup as they wandered from one of the cute stores to another.

At ten, Jasmine arrived. She had already been to the bookstore, and put a bag of books under the counter with her handbag.

Sharon asked, "Did you have any good finds?"

Jasmine smiled, "I've got two Agatha Christies, a Stephen King, a Douglas Adams, and a Terry Pratchett. These will keep me busy all week. You taking your break now?"

"Yeah, Jas, I'll go now, and be back before the lunch rush. I'll just grab a couple of take away coffees, and a biscuit to take with me."

Sharon made herself a cappuccino, and a long black to give away, and put a biscuit in a paper bag. Then she left the shop with Jasmine in charge.

In front of Betsy's Books, she found Carlton, the homeless man who spent his days selling The Big Issue there. Sharon gave him the long black and the biscuit.

"Thanks Shaz," he said. "You know the way to a man's heart."

"No problem. Anything interesting happening in the street today?"

"Nah. It's a quiet day. A couple of people wandering around, not a lot look like they're buying much. Typical mid-week."

"Maybe it'll pick up later. When the people who work on Main Street takes their lunch breaks, a lot of them come down the lane, shopping and getting lunch."

Sharon wandered down the lane, stopping in at the shops, browsing, enjoying the place she'd chosen to have her business. She had been part of the original plans for the Lane. That plan had not just been about the appearance of the lane, and the type of shops that would be there, but also about a culture. Lilly Pilly Lane was not only about being a charming shopping district, but more importantly about being a place where people felt comfortable, safe, and included.

After a half hour walk, she went back to the Bouncing Bean, where a line had formed at the counter. At the front of the line, an older woman was yelling at Jasmine, and demanding to see her manager.

Sharon asked, "What's the problem here?"

"This person..." the woman began.

"I was asking Jasmine," Sharon said.

Jasmine tried to hide her smile, "The customer believes my appearance will affect her coffee. She would like it made by someone else."

Sharon addressed the woman, "That's the problem? You don't want Jasmine to make your coffee?"

"Yes, that's my problem. I don't want this person making my coffee. Look at those piercings. This is not a decent person."

"OK," Sharon said.

"Someone else is making my coffee, then?"

"Sure. Someone else can make your coffee, someone in another coffee shop. You'll find two of them on Main Street."

"You can't tell me to leave. I'm a paying customer."

"Has she paid?"

Jasmine said, "No. We didn't get to her giving her order."

Sharon said, "Then you're not a paying anything, and my customers treat my staff with respect, so you're not a customer. Jasmine, just deal with the next person in line. This woman isn't being served here today."

To the woman, Sharon said, "Please leave. You will be welcome back when your attitude improves."

Jasmine smiled broadly, and took the next person's order. Sharon put her bag behind the counter, washed her hands, and she began to make coffees.

The woman stood, apparently in shock, as other customers went around her to the counter. Eventually, realising everyone was ignoring her, she left.

Later, in a quiet time, Jasmine said, "You could have just made that woman's coffee for her."

"It wasn't worth it. If we allow one person to disrespect a staff member, then people start to think that's acceptable. So we don't. Ever."

Ariana's Cut, Curl and Colour

All of the various businesses in Lilly Pilly Lane always do well. Even in times of economic downturn, when there don't seem to be many customers, the businesses in Lilly Pilly Lane make enough to pay their owners and employees well.

Hardly anyone would suspect some of the success of these many businesses in this charming shopping district could be attributed to the local hairdresser.

At Ariana's Cut, Curl and Colour, customers know Ariana is an excellent hairdresser. Some of them also know she is the world's most powerful witch.

On this day, Carlton, the man who sold The Big Issue in front of the bookshop, looked in at the doorway of the hairdressing salon.

"Hey Ariana, I heard you had a job for me," he said.

"Hi Carlton, yes, I do. How would you like a hundred dollars to get your hair cut?"

"Doesn't it normally work the other way? People pay you? If you start paying people to get their hair cut, that's going to mess up your whole business plan."

Ariana laughed, then explained, "I actually want you to be a model for an assignment my apprentice is doing for her course. Andy needs someone whose hair she can do, and can take photos before and after."

"Oh, I could do that, to help Andy out. You don't need to pay me for that. She's a nice kid. I'd like to help her. Just as long as she doesn't do anything too fancy."

"She's not up to fancy yet. She's just got to demonstrate she can do the basics, wash your hair properly and cut it neatly."

"That's great with me."

"Hey, where are you sleeping lately?"

"Me? You want to come visit?"

Ariana laughed again. She said, "I've got a granny flat, like a studio flat. It's not much, but I don't have a tenant at the moment. It's yours if you want it. Want to take a look?"

"Sure," Carlton answered.

Ariana took a key from a drawer, and led the way around the side of the building. Ariana's business was one of two shopfronts in the street that had residences attached. Ariana lived in the attached house behind the salon. The door she led Carlton, and her assistant Orsinius Wishlet to, was a side door that looked like it might lead into the house.

She opened the door to reveal a large room, with a small kitchenette on one side. In the room was a sofa, television, and coffee table. A door led to a walk-in wardrobe, and a bathroom which also contained a washer and dryer.

"It's all pretty self-contained," Ariana said. "The sofa pulls out into a bed. Let me know if there's anything else you need."

She went to hand him the key. Carlton didn't take it.

He said, "I don't think I can afford it."

"It's free. Think of it as a security thing. Once Orsinius and Andy go home at the end of the day, I'm here alone. Having a man on the property overnight is more secure than just having a woman alone."

Carlton took the key.

"OK," he said. "When do you need me for Andy's project?"

"Can you do nine tomorrow?"

"Sure."

"I've got a customer coming, so Orsinius and I need to get back to the salon. See you tomorrow."

Back in the salon, Orsinius said, "You lied to the old human. You are not safer with him here."

"Carlton is not only an old human but also a proud one. He needs to believe he is somehow paying for what he receives. That's why I told him that him staying here would improve security. It's also why I offered to hire him as a model for a haircut he desperately needs."

"I think I understand. Another thing I did not understand is, I thought that room was just like storage for garden tools. It was not that big."

"I TARDISed it," Ariana said.

"You what?"

"It's a reference to a tv show I used to love as a kid. I made it bigger on the inside than the outside."

"You gave a human a realm key."

"I gave a human a tool shed key. I just sort of overlaid another realm over the tool shed. It will still be that room, no matter who opens the door, or how. The worst I did was unauthorised modification to my house. But no-one's going to know about that, because all the plans of my house are modified to include it. The measurements won't make sense, but anyone who looks at them will believe they make sense."

"That is a lot of magic."

"Not that much. With thought magic. If I can think it, I can make it happen. Don't worry, I won't overdo it and have bad consequences bounce back."

"Then could you do one more piece of magic, please?"

"What's that?"

"It is a long way to move through the Interim to my burrow, and I know you can move there with a thought."

"Why didn't you mention it before? One portal between the salon and your burrow coming up."

"You are a good friend, Ariana."

"So are you, Orsinius."

The Corner Shop

At the Gillard Street end of Lilly Pilly Lane, right on the corner is an old-fashioned corner shop.

It's owned by Petra, and has not changed much since her great-grandparents bought it a hundred years ago. Petra and the corner shop were here before the old dingy shopping street was renamed and revamped. She grew up in the house behind the shop.

Just as her parents, grandparents, and great grandparents did, Petra sells bread, milk, newspapers, and the lollies kids spend their pocket money on. She also stocks breakfast cereals, canned food, some basic deli products and a small amount of fresh fruit. It's not the complete range of a supermarket but, as it's always been, The Corner Shop is where locals know they can duck in quickly for the few odds and ends that aren't worth leaving the neighbourhood.

Her husband Peter lives with her, and occasionally helps her out in the shop. At least twice a day, morning and evening, he leaves to go to the small three hectare allotment he owns to attend to his animals, who belong to his business, Pete's Petting Zoo.

Petra's day begins at five am, when the newspapers arrive, shortly followed by bread and milk deliveries. By six, Pete's made them both breakfast, and they eat together, before he leaves for the farm, and she goes to open the shop. Then she's there for most of the day, taking turns with Pete to break for lunch. For a couple of hours in the afternoon, Pete will be in charge of the shop, while Petra works on the account books for both of their businesses. She takes over the shop again while Pete goes to attend to the animals. At seven pm, she closes the shop, and has dinner with Pete, which he usually will have prepared. It's a long day, but Petra started working in the shop from the time she could walk and talk, so she is used to it.

On this day Petra was munching on toast and jam Pete had brought into the shop for her breakfast, before he went to meet the vet at the farm for annual vaccinations.

It was a busy morning for deliveries, so Petra had no breakfast break, before she opened the shop at seven.

Carlton, the homeless man who spent most of his time in Lilly Pilly Lane, was waiting when she unlocked the shop.

"Hi Pet," he said, cheerily.

"Hi Carlton. What can I do for you today?"

"I want bread, a litre of milk, a couple of cans of baked beans, eggs, and some sliced meat."

"You're sure you want all of that? Have you got a fridge to store things in, somewhere to cook?"

"I have. I've got myself a flat, with a stove and a fridge."

"Hey congratulations. I'll get all your stuff."

"I even have a washing machine now. Oh, that reminds me do you have washing powder?"

"Only one brand, I'm afraid, not much choice."

"I'll take it. Hey, you're still eating breakfast. You do that, I'll get it for myself. Just point me in the right direction."

"Thanks."

Carlton began finding his purchases, and stacking them on the counter.

A delivery driver dropped off a carton of goods.

Carlton accepted the box, and asked Petra where she wanted it.

While she put her plate back in the kitchen another customer came in, and Carlton helped her, to the point where she was ready to check out when Petra returned.

After checking that customer out, Petra looked at Carlton thoughtfully. She said, "You know, normally when Peter's away at meal time, I just don't get to eat. Having you help out was great. Do you want a job? Part time?"

"I'd love a job. When do you want me to start?"

"Looks to me like you already started."

Carlton

It was not quite five in the morning. Carlton left his flat at the side of Ariana's Cut, Curl and Colour. He was eating the last piece of his breakfast toast and Vegemite.

The sky had just a hint of light and the colours of dawn was starting to come through. In the half-dark, he walked up the path to the front of the building.

On the path in front of the salon entrance, a large, glossy, black bird was hopping forward and back, as if he was pacing, waiting for something.

The birds' dawn chorus hadn't started, and to Carlton, it seemed a bit early for day birds like crows to be out, but who knew what went through birds' minds?

"Good morning, crow," he said, "want a bite?"

He broke off a corner of toast and dropped it on the ground.

"Raven," the bird said, looking suspiciously at the toast.

"What?"

"Caw," said the bird, and snapped up the toast.

Carlton shook his head, and continued on his way, not seeing the bird drop the toast and shake his head violently.

He stopped at Knead the Dough Bakery, where the aroma of the morning baking wafted through out. He walked around to the back and knocked. Kaylene came out with a box of fresh-baked, sliced bread.

"Morning, Carlton," she said. "Here's Petra's order. There's a cream bun in there for you as well, to thank you for helping me out with deliveries when Mick was out sick."

"Thanks, but you didn't need to do that. You paid me for my time."

"Yes, but I want you to want to help out next time I'm short-staffed."

"Any time," he laughed, as he left.

He carried the box the rest of the way to the corner of Lilly Pilly Lane and Gillard Street, to The Corner Shop, where he knocked on the door.

Petra was still in her dressing gown as she opened the door. "Hey Carlton," she said. "Pete's spent the night at the property with the vet and Lisa the Llama. She's delivering a breach baby. He's rung me every hour overnight. I'm exhausted. Instead of just covering while I have breakfast, do you mind if I have a nap, as well?"

"Righto. I'll take the deliveries and get ready to open. You have a rest and take over when you're ready."

Carlton stacked the fresh bread in the shelves. He'd just finished when the milk delivery arrived. He received that and signed for it, then stacked the fridge. The papers arrived, dropped on the footpath outside. He brought them in, and put them in their shelves.

Then he went outside again, opened the big sun umbrellas over the outside tables, and cleaned the tables.

By seven he was ready to open up the shop for customers. He heard a mobile phone ring, from in the house end of the building, and Petra talking, though he couldn't make out what she was saying.

A short while later, Petra came into the shop. She said, "We have a new baby llama. Lisa's got a little girl. Pete named her Lyla. Mum and daughter are both doing well."

"Do you want to go meet the new arrival? I can hold the fort here as long as you want," Carlton said.

"Nah, I'm good. You go. If you're not busy, and want to work an extra hour or so, I wouldn't mind you coming back later to give me a lunch break."

Carlton took his paper packet with the cream bun in it and went to the Bouncing Bean coffee shop. He bought two coffees, and walked up the lane to Betsy's Books, where his friend Elizabeth was opening up the shop for the day's business.

They had coffee and cut the cream bun in half to share.

Then he collected his chair and bundle of magazines from Elizabeth's store cupboard, where he'd begun keeping them, and set up outside.

When he'd first started selling The Big Issue in Lilly Pilly Lane, Carlton had had no home, no job, and no friends. Now, he'd found all three. He felt happy, and at home.

Quoth the Raven

When Ariana unlocked the front door of the hairdressing salon, she found Corvin Ravenwing pacing, with his hopping gait on the front path.

"Lady Ariana," he greeted her.

"Hello Corvin. Good to see you. Would you like to come in."

"Yes. I would like to come in. A human gave me a piece of his food. We should dispose of that." He indicated with his beak to a small piece of toast.

Ariana picked it up. "I see you've met Carlton," she said. "Although, if you were here when he left for the day, you've been here for hours."

"I have."

"You could have tried tapping on the door or a window."

"I did not want to presume."

"Corvin, you don't need stand on ceremony. We're friends."

"Are we?" Corvin was once more overwhelmed with the way such a powerful being so casually treated lesser creatures as equals.

"Of course. Come on in and tell me what's bothering you."

As they sat down in the salon break room, Ariana on a chair, and Corvin on the table, Orsinius Wishlet walked through a wall and joined them.

Corvin jumped in surprise.

"It's just a portal," Ariana said. "It makes it easier for Orsinius to get to work."

Corvin had a slight quaver to his voice. "Lady Ariana, it pains me to say this."

"What's wrong."

"You may recall that awful time Mordred put that collar on me."

"Yes, I remember."

"And you saved me, and destroyed the collar to free me."

"Yes."

"Then you and the others chased Mordred through the Interim."

"Yes."

"And I stayed with that man who'd also been trapped in a collar, who you also helped, Mr Jack Jones."

"Did Jack do something to harm you?"

"No... but... I... told him he could call me if he needed legal advice."

"And he called you?"

"I can't tell you."

"OK. If he isn't a client, you can tell me that, but if he is a client, you can't tell me. He wants you to do something with regard to me, because otherwise you wouldn't need to warn me about it, which of course you're not doing because you're not telling me anything."

"I have to go to see Lady Justice today."

"Lady Justice has given him an order keeping him away from me. He wants you to apply to have the order overturned."

"Such orders have never happened in the magical world before.They belong in human law, not ours."

"The alternative was that she was going to remove his head. She's been adapting things from human law, to reduce the number of heads she removes."

Corvin shook again. "It is a most unusual thing."

"But you can't tell me if Jack's your client, and if it's about that. Good to know."

"You must understand, Lady Ariana. I do not wish to do anything to harm you."

"Don't worry Corvin. I know you have a job to do. I'm pretty sure Lady Justice won't go back on her order, but even if she does, I can deal with Jack. You go ahead, and do the job you've got to do. And thank you for coming to not tell me what it's about."

Corvin bowed down low. He said, "You are most gracious Lady Ariana. I promise in future I will be more careful who I accept as a client."

"So you're dealing with scumbags, never more?"

"I do not understand what you mean."

"Don't worry about it. Do you want me to transport you to Lady Justice?"

Corvin looked anxiously at the blank wall Orsinius had just appeared through. He said, "I think I will take the Interim. Thank you for your kindness.

Hearing

They met in a large room in Lady Justice's house.

Lady Justice began, the record being magically written in one of her large books.

"The complainant in this matter is Mr Jack Jones. He is being represented by solicitor Mr Corvin Ravenwing. The respondent is Lady Ariana Sutton, who is represented by Merlin the Wizard. Merlin, while not technically a solicitor, was present for the creation of most magical law, and so this court recognises him as qualified. Also present for these proceedings are the Junior Justice, Andromeda, and Mr Orsinius Wishlet, Guardian of Mythical Objects. These two are present to witness justice done. Ariadne, nine hundred and fifty-sixth Lady Justice presiding."

Lady Justice continued. "As Mr Jones has brought these actions, Mr Ravenwing, would you please state your case."

Corvin Ravenwing, began, hesitatingly. "Lady Justice, as you are aware Mr Jones and Lady Ariana were once married under human law. They were subsequently divorced under human law. That is not the business of this court, of course. However, they have never been divorced under magical law, and it has come to Mr Jones' attention that Lady Ariana is a magical being, and therefore he believes that he is still married to Lady Ariana under magical law. He further believes that," here Corvin cringed, "if she requires a divorce under magical law, he is entitled to half of all of her possessions, including her magical power."

"Your response, Merlin?"

"Quite simple, Your Ladyship," Merlin said. "They were never married under magical law. Lady Ariana had no idea she was a magical being at the time, and Mr Jones had not revealed that he was one to her. Even then, under human law, Lady Ariana sought the divorce at the earliest possible opportunity after the marriage, as she discovered it was entered into under false pretences. If he now claims it was a marriage under magical law, that was also entered into under false pretences. If you add that to the recent harassment of Lady Ariana, and both during and after the time he was with The Power, Mr Jones has proven himself to be a self-serving, dishonest person. This is an attempt to use the law to get what he was unable to do by manipulation, direct theft, malicious misuse of magic, and other means. It is part of a continuing pattern of harassment that every person in this room is aware of. I believe granting Mr Jones' request would set a very bad precedent in magical law."

Lady Justice looked at Corvin, "Do you have any response to that."

Corvin bowed low, and said, "I have nothing to add, Your Ladyship."

Lady Justice took a deep breath, then released it slowly.

"Mr Jones has been given opportunities, time and time again to reform. As Merlin has pointed out, attempts to steal Lady Ariana's magic have been a major part of his reprehensible behaviour. His co-conspirator in the original misuse of magic charge, where Lady Ariana was trapped in the Interim by malicious misuse of magic, was executed at the time of the offence. I now regret having failed to impose the same penalty on Mr Jones as soon as his part in the crime came to light. Until now, there has only ever been one penalty for the malicious misuse of magic. While I tried to take into account extenuating circumstances, those circumstances do not excuse his continued behaviour. So now, I will impose the penalty I ought to have imposed originally."

The movement was faster than anyone could see. Lady Justice pulled the Sword of Justice from under her left wing, and swiped, beheading Jack in one smooth motion.

His head fell to the floor moments before his body slumped.

Everyone else in the room stared in shock.

Lady Justice said, "Let the record state that the only recognised penalty for the malicious misuse of magic has been imposed. While this court has found there are things to be learned from the human justice system, there are some areas where the established practice of magical law must hold sway."

Anxious Andy

The weight of destiny hung heavily on the three people who worked at Ariana's Cut, Curl and Colour.

Ariana herself had not known until her early twenties that she already had a huge amount of magical power, but, shortly after discovering that, was destined to become the world's most powerful witch, through gaining the power of an ancestor.

Orsinius Wishlet had begun life, as many wisps did, as a petty thief, yet the wizard Merlin had said he would become something more, and Orsinius was now Guardian of Mythical Objects.

The youngest of the group, Andromeda Justice, had only discovered the day after her sixteenth birthday that she was not human, but was destined to be arbiter of all magical justice, as her mother currently was. On the day before this one, she had witnessed her first execution, which she had been unprepared for.

Andy, Ariana and Orsinius sat together in the break room, having their coffee before starting work.

They were all still in shock from the way the previous day's legal hearing had ended.

Andy said, "I know that's my mother's job, but, actually seeing it…"

Ariana said, "I know. I've seen it three times now. I still can't … after my sister, I didn't sleep for a week, I just kept seeing that sword."

"I also see the sword in my mind all the time," Orsinius said, taking a huge gulp of his coffee. "That is why I stopped being a thief after your sister …"

Ariana said, "I understand. It was frightening, terrifying."

"I don't think I can do it, take over from my mother, I mean," Andy said. "I can't cut people's heads off. Why should I have to?"

"I don't know why," Ariana said. "You shouldn't have to. You should have a choice, but I'm not sure you do. Maybe you're supposed to not want it. Someone who really wanted the job, who wanted to be the final arbiter of all magical justice, who had the power to decide on execution and just do it - I think someone who really wanted all that power would be the worst possible person to have it."

Andy said, "So who should do it? Someone who doesn't want to do it? Why does that someone have to be me?"

Ariana shook her head, "I don't know, Andy. This is the type of thing you need to talk to your mother about. She must have gone through this when she first saw her mother in action. Maybe that's why you're not supposed to take over until you're a hundred, so you have time to deal with all of this. It's pretty big stuff. I don't know how I would handle it if I was in your shoes. But your mum's been changing it as well, she's introduced imprisonment and probation, avoiding execution where she can. Maybe when you get the job, if you get the job, you can do it without the execution part."

"I'm studying law part-time, because Mum wants me to," Andy said, "and I'm studying the family records, all because Mum says I should. Really all I want to do is work here, do my hairdressing apprenticeship, and just live like a normal person. Is that too much to want? I don't want to decide who's right and who's wrong, and cut people's heads off."

"That seems reasonable to me," Ariana said.

"Has any Junior Justice ever refused to become Lady Justice? Orsinius asked, wonder in his voice. "I have not heard of it. It seems impossible."

"No. Not ever," Andy said. "But my mother let me believe I was human until I was sixteen. None of the others did that. I know that there's another life possible, not just this messed up destiny stuff."

Orsinius was thoughtful. "If you do not do it, there will be no Lady Justice. Magical law will disappear."

"Maybe," Ariana said, "or maybe in a hundred years, the magical world will have to find another way to deal with justice matters. Talk with your mother, Andy. Actually tell her how you're feeling. "

"Yeah," Andy said, "I will."

"Do you want to take the day off, today? Yesterday was pretty intense."

"No. I want to work. I want to feel normal."

The Talk

I knew it was coming, the talk. I knew it, because I'd had the same talk with my own mother, at the same age, after my own similar first experience.

I didn't push for it. I knew it had to happen in Andy's own time, just as it had happened in mine.

I hadn't really had anyone to talk to before I had the talk with my mother. Andy had Ariana and Orsinius. I could be jealous, but they have been friends to me when I have needed them as well.

Andy and I sat at the kitchen table, with mugs of hot chocolate, and she asked, "Has anyone ever refused the role of Lady Justice?"

"No, but I think all of us have considered refusing it. I considered it when I was your age. My mother told me she did, too."

"But you did it."

"When you're a teenager, and you're trying to come to terms with this, is very different from when you're a hundred and it's time to actually take over the role. Destiny's like that. You have to grow into it. It wasn't all that long ago your wings started to grow in, and you didn't want that, didn't want to be different. You didn't think you'd accept your wings, but now you've grown into them. You're used to them. You don't think twice about covering them with a glamour when you're going to be among humans, and you can even use them to fly … passably … You'll get better."

I'd got a smile from her. I hadn't seen her smile since Jack's execution. I supposed the talk was going well. Then she went on to the next question, the one I had also asked at her age.

"Do we have to execute people? I mean, you've tried imprisonment with Lord Rust, and you imposed a restraining order on Jack, but then you went back on it and just ..."

"I had to execute him. I gave him chances, but he kept disobeying the law, pushing back against every rule."

"But wasn't there something else that could be done?"

"I'd already done the worst thing possible, let him live after discovering he'd been involved in the malicious misuse of magic. We can't let people who misuse magic live, it's too dangerous. Our people, the people of the magical world, could destroy the whole world of mundane humans if we chose to. Ariana's ancestor almost destroyed reality. She tore a hole in this Reality, and another and somehow began to merge the two. If Orsinius and Ariana hadn't managed to close that rip, the world we know would have ceased to exist. Magic is dangerous. We control it, or it gets out of hand. The only way we can truly stop someone who is determined to misuse magic, is execution. That's why we do it. Time and again, our ancestors have considered alternatives, but then come back to having to impose the same, horrible, penalty. None of us have ever liked it, or wanted to do it, but it's necessary."

"Ariana said she thought someone who actually wanted the job was probably not someone who was suitable for it."

"Ariana was right. This is a responsibility to be carried as a heavy weight, not as a joy. And, executions, are sadly a necessary part of that heavy weight."

Then Andy asked the question that had not been part of the conversation when I'd had it with my mother, to my knowledge, a question never asked in our family history.

"So if execution's the only solution to malicious magic, what do we do when they come back?"

Emergency Meeting

Everyone who had been at Jack's hearing gathered together in the break room of Ariana's hairdressing salon.

Andy looked down at her hands, while everyone else looked at her.

Ariana said, gently, "It's OK. We can help. Just tell us what happened."

Andy looked up, eyes holding tears hadn't quite escaped to roll down her face, but were about to do so.

She looked around the group of concerned adults: her mother Lady Justice, the famous wizard Merlin, the solicitor Corvin Ravenwing, her mentor, the witch Ariana, and Orsinius Wishlet, the wisp, reformed thief, and guardian of Mythical Objects. These adults were her friends, who were all concerned about her.

She began her story, "After the hearing... After Mr Jones was executed... That night..." She stopped.

Lady Justice said, "Go on. You can tell us anything."

The tears began to escape, as Andy spoke, haltingly, "That night... I woke up, and heard his voice... Mr Jones... It was like he was right in my ear... He said... He said... If my mother could take his life... If my mother could take his life, he could take what she valued... After that... I was woken every night... Sometimes, I saw him... Sometimes, I just heard him... After a week..."

She stopped talking, and pushed up the long sleeves on her dress. Over her arms were bruises, cuts, and some definite bite marks.

Lady Justice hugged her daughter.

Ariana said, "This can't go on. We have to find a way to exorcise or banish or whatever you do to a malevolent ghost, and in the meantime, we have to protect Andy at all costs."

Merlin said, "I concur. We must also consider that if we can deny him access to Miss Andromeda, he might attack any one of us. We should all be on alert at all times."

"I believe we want a safe house," Ariana said.

She opened a door which normally connected her business to her residence, but now opened on to a completely different space, the realm she had inherited from Lady Arabella March. The others followed her in.

It seemed less cluttered than in the past. The room the door led to was now a cosy lounge area with a fire place, bookshelves, and comfortable lounge chairs.

"I've made some changes," Ariana said. "After Merlin and I finished our inventory, we put all the really nasty stuff in the room with the red door, until we work out how to destroy it safely. Most of the other magical stuff is in a new workroom, and store room. I've also added a kitchen, and some comfortable bedrooms. Admittedly, I added those other things as we came through the door. Combining thought magic with an infinite space and infinite possibilities can give us anything we need."

She opened a drawer in what looked like an antique sideboard, and took out five gold keys.

"Realm keys? You have multiple keys for this same realm?" Corvin was still learning that unheard of things simply happened with this group of people.

"I do for now," Ariana said. I'm giving you each a key. This is our safe house, the place to retreat to if you feel you are in any danger. I'd also recommend that Andy sleeps here at night, and at least one of us stays with her each night." Ariana handed out the keys.

As Corvin received his gold key, he recalled giving Ariana an identical key and having to explain its purpose and means of use. Then, powerful witch that she was, she immediately changed how it was used.

Ariana said, "I guess I don't have to tell anyone here to be very careful that no-one gets hold of these keys. I'll take them back once this is over. I trust everyone here, but I would hate to think what would happen if one of these keys was stolen, especially if it happened before Merlin and I could work out what to do with everything behind the red door."

Andy asked, "Is there internet access here?"

Ariana thought for a moment, then said, "There is now."

Andy said, "So I could just stay here when I'm not at work, and do my classes online."

Ariana said, "You could, if that's what you want."

Merlin said, "I suspect that the answer to the question of how to banish the ghost might be in the books Lady Arabella left."

Ariana said, "I've added a library. Lady Arabella's books are there. The books in here are from my own collection, mostly fiction."

Merlin said, "Then I suggest you and I scour the library, and whatever spells and potions you have in your work room, store room, and even the room with the red door. We cannot leave the Junior Justice under threat."

Lady Justice said, "I will consult Benwyn, Claire, and other magical practitioners to see if any of those have experience in banishing ghosts."

Orsinius said, "I will go and see if Augustus has anything in his shop which might help with this, or if he is able to obtain anything."

Corvin looked around the group. Everyone, except him, seemed to have a purpose toward solving the problem.

Ariana noticed his gaze. "Corvin, I expect that, as a lawyer, you have some skills in administration, and keeping track of information. Could you please be our contact point? We can each tell you what we've found, or failed to find, and you can keep the whole group informed?"

Corvin gratefully accepted his role.

Ariana took the gold butterfly brooch from her own blouse and pinned it to Andy's dress.

"Another level of protection," Ariana said.

Sword of Justice

Account of the execution of the ghosts of two previously-executed criminals.

In the quest to banish the ghost which had been attacking the Junior Justice Andromeda, we each had our own assignments.

The Wizard Merlin and Lady Ariana had found spells for summoning a ghost, and binding one. Those spells were in an old and damaged book, among the books left by Lady Arabella March, so we were unsure of their effectiveness.

I'd obtained from Claire of Canterbury a spell for banishing a ghost. The spell was from memory, as her books had long been lost, and she was not certain of it.

As we found each spell and reported to Corvin Ravenwing, he'd despatched Orsinius Wishlet, Guardian of Mythical Objects, to acquire the items we would need. Mr Ravenwing never left Andromeda alone while we all did our research, for which I am grateful.

We gathered in Lady Ariana's realm, the "safe house" as we were considering it, to discuss where we would summon the ghost of her ex-husband.

Lady Ariana recommended that we leave Mr Ravenwing and Andromeda in the safe house, and perform the summoning ritual elsewhere, in case something went wrong.

Merlin suggested the cave where we had found, and executed Mordred, the last known remnant of the organisation known as The Power.

We left Mr Ravenwing and Andromeda, with Lady Ariana's butterfly brooch in the safe house. Mr Wishlet brought a bag, in which he had put a thermos of coffee, and the mythical objects under his protection, as well as the objects needed for the rituals, and we were ready to leave.

Lady Ariana used her thought magic to transport the four of us to the cave.

There Merlin drew a circle on the floor, and Lady Ariana laid out objects for the summoning ritual. We chanted the words of the ritual and called on the ghost of Jack Jones who appeared in the centre of the circle.

Lady Ariana swiftly added the items for the binding spell, and we moved into that.

I asked the ghost why he had attacked my child. He yelled, "It wasn't me!" He began to writhe and struggle, pulling at something on his neck.

Mr Wishlet pulled forth Excalibur, and struck at the ghost's neck, which revealed a ghost version of the golden collars The Power used to enslave its victims.

Lady Ariana grabbed the ethereal collar, and it crumbled, just as the real one that had held him enthralled in life, had done.

We then moved into the banishment ceremony, and nothing happened. It failed.

The ghost began to laugh and Lady Ariana said, "Your sword Lady Justice."

I drew my sword to find it glowing red. I swung and the ghost's head fell off before it disappeared.

My sword returned to its normal appearance.

"Did you do that?" I asked Lady Ariana.

She said she had not.

Merlin suggested that the Sword of Justice might be designed to adapt to whatever offender was being punished.

We had begun to pack up, when Lady Ariana stood suddenly still, then said, "It's not over. The butterfly's calling."

She transported us immediately to the safe house, where we found the Andromeda crying, sitting on the floor, leaning against the red door, behind which the worst of the deceased Lady Arabella March's magical items had been confined. Mr Ravenwing was lying injured on the floor, a wing and his beak both broken. The gold butterfly was also bent and broken.

Andromeda said, "I heard a knock at the door, and thought one of you had forgotten to bring your key. I opened the door and a ghost came in. It wasn't Mr Jones. It was another ghost. He said he'd come for me. The butterfly and Corvin, both fought him back, and when he was up against the red door it just opened and he fell in and it closed again. I think the butterfly did it, with Ariana's magic. But it's broken now, and Corvin's hurt, and the ghost's in there where all the bad stuff is locked away." She was crying so much she was coughing and hiccuping.

It was terrible to see my child in that state, and my friend injured, but there was work to be done.

Merlin raised his staff, and the red door opened. The ghost of Mordred rushed out. I used my sword, which was again glowing red, and dispatched it in an instant. The sword then returned to its normal state.

Merlin entered the room to ensure there was no dangerous spells released.

I stooped to comfort Andromeda, and to find that she was not physically hurt.

Mr Wishlet had taken the grail from his bag, and poured coffee from the thermos into it. In an earlier adventure he and Lady Ariana had found that the mildly magical liquid acted as a carrier for the power of the grail. Lady Ariana rushed to her work room and came back with an eyedropper. She used it to feed coffee from the grail to Mr Ravenwing. As we watched, his wing regained its shape and his broken beak regrew.

Once he was recovered, Lady Ariana told him she would make him a salve to apply to his injuries if they gave him any pain.

Andromeda exclaimed her sadness at the broken butterfly.

Lady Ariana said it had done its job, and she could create another if needed. We all knew, however, that this particular brooch had a sentimental significance to her before she had applied magic to it, and we felt for her loss.

Mr Wishlet picked up the broken butterfly and dropped it into the dregs of the coffee in the grail.

Moments later, it flew free, restored, and alighted on Lady Ariana's blouse, to attach itself like an ordinary brooch once more. Lady Ariana was very thankful.

Once more, I must commend my companions in this endeavour. Without their help justice may not have been done, and the ghostly attacks on the Junior Justice might have continued.

Ariadne, Nine Hundred and Fifty-sixth Lady Justice.

Celebration

Ariana had received the telepathic message from Benwyn, asking her to gather their friends together, as he and Claire wished for them to meet the new baby.

The break room of the salon didn't seem appropriate for the gathering, so she used the break room door to open her inherited realm.

There, with a little thought magic, she expanded the cosy lounge and dining areas, and cooked a feast.

She'd become so used to this space, now that she'd stamped her own personality on it, and put the worst of Lady Arabella's nasty magical items out of sight, that she was more and more considering living it in instead of the house attached to the salon.

She left that doorway open, as Lady Justice and Andy arrived, shortly followed by Merlin and Orsinius Wishlet.

"I told Benwyn we'd meet in the break room, but I thought this would be nicer," Ariana said.

The others agreed it was definitely nicer.

Not long after they were all settled, the bell on the salon door rang, and then Benwyn arrived in the room carrying a swaddled bundle.

"Claire is just behind me," he said. He unwrapped the cloth to reveal a scruffy black kitten with big blue eyes.

Ariana gasped, and the others stared, all recalling that Benwyn had been a sleek, black cat for so long.

Then the door bell rang again, followed by Claire entering the room. Clair was in a long, flowing white gown, carrying a baby who wore a similar gown, which flowed over Claire's arm.

Claire and Benwyn both looked at the expressions on their friends' faces and laughed.

Benwyn said, "We gave a home to a cat who had kittens. Since my resuming my true form deprived you of a cat, Ariana, I thought you might like this little girl." He passed the kitten to Ariana. It scrambled up her arm, perched on her shoulder, and bathed itself, purring.

Benwyn continued, "Now, my friends, Claire and I would like to introduce you to another little girl. We named her after the wisest and strongest women we know. Please meet Ariana Ariadne Andromeda Canterbury."

"That name's a mouthful," Ariana said, "but I am so honoured."

"As am I," Lady Justice said.

Andy asked, "I get why you named her after Ariana and Mum, but why me?"

Benwyn smiled at the teenager, "Andy, you know I have the limited gift of foresight. You have only lived a fifth of a fifth of your life, so you are just beginning on your path. I have seen just a little of the woman you will be. Under the influence of your mother and your mentor, you will be a woman equal to any, and greater than many, in power, in wisdom, and in compassion. You will be a woman whose name I would like my daughter to grow into."

Claire asked Lady Justice if she would formally record the baby's name in the official records, and if everyone present would stand as godparents, and offer a blessing.

Lady Justice began, "Ariana Ariadne Andromeda, may your thoughts and words be wise, and your path through life be honest, may you always have all you need."

She gave the baby a silver rattle, shaped like a gavel.

Merlin said, "Little child, may you always have an enquiring mind, be willing to learn new things, and to know enough to know when you do not know enough."

He gave the child a crystal ball, that would mutate into a globe, or a nightlight, at a touch.

Andy said, "Little Ariana, whatever your destiny is, I hope you will be brave, and that people who love you will help." She gave the baby a doll, dressed in medieval costume, which looked like Claire.

Ariana said, "May you always have friends who will help you with the challenges of life, and who you will help in turn." She took the gold butterfly brooch off her own blouse, whispered something to it, and held it out on her flat hand. She said, "And may you always be safe from all dangers. This gift is for protection and companionship, and a reassurance that help is available at a moment's notice, if you ever need it."

The butterfly flapped its wings and flew to the baby. Baby Ariana laughed as the butterfly flew gracefully around her head. It alighted on Claire's dress, close to the baby, but just out of reach.

Orsinius said, "I do not know much about words, and blessings. I promise to be a friend to you, if you wish it. I hope you discover what things have value and what things do not, and especially the value of the magic that happens when you have friends. I have a gift for you too. I understand it is of monetary value, and might help you at some time in your life."

He held a ruby the size of a golf ball, that until now had been kept in the deepest part of his burrow on the border between Reality and Unreality. He held it up for the baby to see the sparkle, then gave the jewel to Benwyn.

Benwyn looked at the ruby intently, then said, "I know this jewel. It belonged to my father all those years ago. He kept it in an old chest, under his bed. I would have inherited it, along with the rest of the estate, had things not gone as they did. It's so fitting it's come back to the family line. I will look after it for her. Orsinius, this is an amazing gift."

A large black bird stepped out of the Interim, dragging a paper-wrapped parcel, by the string that held the wrapping together. He was clearly struggling with it.

Ariana said, "Benwyn, I think you met Corvin in passing, the night we caught Mordred. Let me introduce you properly. Lord Benwyn and Lady Claire of Canterbury, meet Mr Corvin Ravenwing. Corvin is a bird of many talents, not the least of which being that he is a skilled solicitor. I hired him on your behalf, Claire."

Claire said, "On my behalf? What for?"

Corvin answered, "Lady Ariana instructed me to, if possible, locate and acquire some of your property, to whit, your books of magic. I ascertained that three books which had belonged to one Claire of Canterbury, a witch executed in your time, were in existence, at the British Museum. These books were not in the museum display, but in storage. I negotiated the return with the museum's legal representative. That person was very disturbed to be arguing the matter with a talking bird, but I have encountered such prejudice before and insisted continuing the negotiations. I argued that as the legal owner of these books was alive, not deceased as their records said, the books should be considered stolen, and must be returned. When that argument failed, I offered a trade of some gold bars, supplied by Lady Ariana from her inheritance, which were forged three hundred years ago. As those had both historic and monetary value, the museum agreed to the trade. So I am able to return three books to you. My enquiries have not located any others still in existence."

Corvin took a deep breath after his speech.

"My books?"

"Shall I hold the baby while you open the parcel, and check on them?" Lady Justice offered.

Claire passed baby Ariana to her, so she could unwrap the books. The butterfly followed its tiny new mistress.

Claire ran her hands over the books, and flicked through the aging pages.

"I don't know how to thank you, Corvin, or you Ariana, for getting these back to me. ... Oh, here's why that banishment spell didn't work, Lady Justice, I had it wrong. ... This means so much. And now I'm going to be able to teach this to little Ariana. She's going to know her family tradition. This means more than I can tell you."

Claire was almost in tears looking at her lost books. Benwyn put his arm around her.

"Truly, we have great friends," he said.

"More friends are coming," Ariana said.

Queen Rose of the fairies soon arrived with the Princess Aster, and Primrose, the nursery maid and official Hero. Queen Rose declared the baby would be, as her father was, a friend to all of the fae. Princess Aster insisted she and baby Ariana were going to be best friends. She also asked Benwyn to do his turning into a cat trick once more.

Last to the party was Augustus Wishlet, who had been a prior owner of Benwyn in his cat form.

The friends talked long into the night, recalling past adventures, sharing a meal, and taking turns to hold the newest member of their circle.

The kitten, after tiring of her perch on Ariana's shoulder, explored the realm, and the salon, before returning to curl up on Ariana's lap. Like everyone else there, she knew she belonged.